What's a serious detective like me doing in such a silly movie?

What's a serious detective like me doing in such a silly movie?

LINDA BAILEY

KIDS CAN PRESS

First U.S. edition 2003

This is a work of fiction and any resemblance of characters to persons living or dead is
purely coincidental.

Many of the designations used by manufacturers and sellers to distinguish their
products are claimed as trademarks. Where those designations appear in this book and
Kids Can Press Ltd. was aware of a trademark claim, the designations have been printed
in initial capital letters (e.g., Golden Globe).

Kids Can Press acknowledges the financial support of the Ontario Arts Council, the
Canada Council for the Arts and the Government of Canada, through the BPIDP, for
our publishing activity.

Published in Canada by
Kids Can Press Ltd.
29 Birch Avenue
Toronto, ON M4V 1E2

Published in the U.S. by
Kids Can Press Ltd.
2250 Military Road
Tonawanda, NY 14150

www.kidscanpress.com

Edited by Charis Wahl
Cover designed by Julia Naimska
Typeset by Rachel Di Salle
Printed and bound in Canada

CM 03 0 9 8 7 6 5 4 3 2 1
CM PA 02 0 9 8 7 6 5 4 3 2

National Library of Canada Cataloguing in Publication Data

Bailey, Linda, 1948–
  What's a serious detective like me doing in such a silly movie

(A Stevie Diamond mystery)
ISBN 1-55074-926-9 (bound).   ISBN 1-55074-922-6 (pbk.)

I. Title. II. Series: Bailey, Linda, 1948–   .
Stevie Diamond mysteries.

PS8553.A3644W384 2002   jC813'.54   C2001-904242-6
PZ7.B1526Wf 2002

Kids Can Press is a *Corus*™ Entertainment company

**To my great friend and valued
writing buddy, Deborah Hodge**

Thanks go to Katie Keating and her dad,
Fred Keating, as well as to the cast and crew
of *Due East* for their help with research.
Thanks also to Maurice Verkaar for his
helpful critique of the manuscript.

CHAPTER

There they were — nine words I'd waited my whole life to hear.

"How would you like to be in a movie?"

I was holding the phone so tight I'm surprised the plastic didn't snap. At the other end of the line was Gertie Wiggins, my neighbor. Gertie's an actor, and she knows a lot of people in the movie business here in Vancouver. For months, she'd been promising to get me a job in the movies.

And here it was. My big break! My foot in the door! One thing would lead to another, and before you could say "Academy Award nomination," I'd be launched on a fantastic new career.

I know what you're thinking. It's not easy to become a movie star. Well, it's not easy to become a kid detective either, and somehow I'd managed that.

I'm Stevie (short for Stephanie) Diamond, and the truth is, I got into detecting through pure dumb luck. On my first case, I just *happened* to be in the right place at the right time when a thousand bucks got stolen. On my second case, I stumbled into a smuggling ring. After that, the mysteries just started dropping into my lap ... a third, fourth, fifth, sixth. It was like I was Nancy Drew!

I figured it could be the same with the movies. All I needed was a lucky break.

"Hot dog!" I said. "Where do I go? What do I do?"

"Whoa," said Gertie. "You have to get hired first. It's a horror film called *Night of the Neems*. They need lots of kids."

"Neems? What's a neem?"

"Haven't a clue," said Gertie. "Your first step is to sign up at the T-for-Talent Agency. Tell them I sent you. As an extra."

"An extra?" I slumped a little. "Does that mean I don't get to say anything?"

"Extras stay in the background."

"Sure, fine. But I get to say *something*, don't I?"

"Not a word. That's why you're extra." There was a pause. "Nobody starts at the top, Stevie."

I nodded into the phone. "Got it. Stay in the background."

For about a day, I thought. They'd be sure to notice me after a day.

"They want boys, too," said Gertie. "Can you tell Jesse?"

"Sure." Jesse Kulniki's my friend and neighbor. Also my detecting partner. Those six mysteries I mentioned? He was there all the way. Diamond & Kulniki — that's us. I wouldn't dream of becoming a movie star without Jesse.

Gertie asked to speak to my mom. I handed the phone over and raced around the corner to Jesse's house. He was sitting cross-legged on the living-room rug, hunched over a book the size of a small raft.

"How would you like to be in a movie?" I asked.

"Just a second, Stevie. Let me write this down." He scribbled something in a notebook.

Didn't he *hear* me?

"A movie," I repeated. "Big screen! Theaters across the nation! People lining up for our autographs!"

"Almost done," he mumbled. I glanced at the page he was reading. It was covered with skinny long-legged birds.

"But —"

"Sshhh!" He held up a hand, palm out. It was covered in ink stains.

I waited, staring at the part in his straight brown hair. It took him a good *three minutes* to get done! I couldn't believe it.

"There," he said finally, dropping his pen and stretching. "What's up? You want to go to a movie?"

"Not *go* to a movie! *Be* in a movie! *Night of the Neems!*"

"What's a neem?" asked Jesse.

"I don't know. It doesn't matter. The point is, we can be in it!" I told him about Gertie's call.

"I don't think so." He reached for his pen.

"WHAT?"

"It'll take too much time. I've got stuff to do."

"What stuff?" Was he crazy?

He pointed at the giant book. "My science-fair project, for one thing."

"Jesse Kulniki, you would actually give up a

chance to be in a movie for a bunch of dumb storks?"

He frowned. "They're not dumb. And they're not storks, either. They're herons. They just look like storks because —"

My eyes rolled back in my head. "Who the heck cares?"

He didn't answer.

Uh-oh ... Jesse can get a little weird on the subject of birds. In most ways, he's a totally regular guy. But get to know him better, and you'll find out about the binoculars (three pairs!) on the windowsills of his room, pointing outside, just in case. You'll spot the bird stuff on his dresser — crumbling nests, broken eggshells, boxes of feathers. The guy *definitely* has birds on the brain. Be careful how you say that, though. He doesn't like "birdbrain" at all.

In the end, I promised to help him with his project, which mostly seemed to involve going down to the beach and watching storks — sorry, herons — while they stood on one leg and stared at the water. Jesse planned to observe herons for at least thirty hours, which sounded to me like a serious put-yourself-to-sleep project. But the trade was that he'd be in the movie, so it was worth it.

I headed home in a great mood. Jesse and I were going to have a fantastic time and probably end up movie stars, too.

My mom and dad were sitting at the kitchen table. Was it my imagination, or did they look guilty?

"Um, Stevie?" said my mom. "Look, hon, we're sorry. We know the movies must seem glamorous ..."

Yup, they did look guilty.

She stared at her fingernails. "We don't think this movie job is going to work out."

I sat down and lay my forehead on the table. That stopped them.

After a minute, my dad said, "Don't be like this, Stevie."

"Like what?" I stared at the wood grain of the table. "Why can't I be in *Night of the Neems*?"

"Is that what it's called?" asked my mom.

"What's a neem?" asked my dad.

I let out a sigh and sat up. "Give me one good reason why I can't be in the movie."

"We'll give you three," said my dad. "Number one, school. Gertie says this would be a couple of weeks full time. That's a lot of school to miss."

My mom jumped in. "Number two, child extras need an adult with them on set. Gertie said so. We can't take time off work, and neither can Jesse's mom — and Gertie's rehearsing a play. There's no one to chaperone you and Jesse."

"Number three," said my dad, holding up three fingers just in case I'd lost count. "Gram Diamond. She's arriving tomorrow for a visit, remember? And you know what *that's* like."

This was the big one. Gram Diamond is my dad's mother. She's what my mother calls "a force." I'm not sure what a force is, but I think it's something like a tornado or a hurricane. That's definitely what it feels like when Gram visits.

"We'll have enough to cope with ..." said my mom, her voice getting a little shrill. She cleared her throat before continuing, "... without you in the movies."

I laid my forehead back down on the table. This wouldn't be easy. My mom gets kind of rattled around Gram Diamond, and she counts on me to keep Gram busy. Gram and I are pretty good together. When I'm not feeling blown over by her, she can be kind of fun.

Well, okay. Maybe fun is going too far.

"Stevie?" said my dad. "Are you all right?" He *sounded* guilty, too.

"I'm fine," I said, thinking hard. I was pretty sure I could get around missing school — my marks were good. But the chaperone thing and the Gram Diamond problem were tougher. Not impossible — nothing's impossible for a detective and soon-to-be movie star. But tougher.

Sitting up, I stared at my parents. "Okay."

"Okay?" They both said it at the same time in *exactly* the same surprised voice.

I nodded. My mom's mouth dropped open. My dad blinked in confusion. Good. Keep them on their toes.

"I guess I'd better do my homework."

As I walked up the stairs, my mom's voice drifted up behind me. "There's always next time." It was that cheery, chirpy Mom voice — the one they use when they're trying to make you feel better.

Right.

In my room, I started pacing. For reasons I don't understand, my brain seems to be connected to my feet. I think better if my feet are moving. Unfortunately, pacing my room is a challenge. It's not that the room's too small. It's just that the floor's a little lumpy. Dirty clothes, damp towels, overdue library books, bowls of old popcorn, half-finished model of an ancient Egyptian town (which, if you're thinking of trying it, is *way* too hard to make), bag of cat food —

"Rowwrrr!"

Cat.

"Sorry." I lifted my foot. Giving me a hurt look, Radical slunk away.

"I really am sorry."

I cleared a short path and started pacing again. Simple problem solving, that's what this was, just like solving a crime. I started with the chaperone. Jesse and I needed an adult with nothing in the world to do except hang around with us. Tough one.

I was concentrating so hard I didn't even hear the phone ring. My mom's voice floated up the stairs, still sounding guilty-chirpy. "Stevie? It's Gram Diamond on the line. She wants to speak to you."

I picked up the extension in my parents' room. Gram launched right in. "So, Stevie-girl, I bought you some terrific books at The Book Bin, the kind you like, mysteries. I hope you haven't read them, but I wanted to check, because I could return them tomorrow. The Book Bin opens at ten, and I'll have plenty of time because my flight doesn't go till the afternoon."

She went on, telling me the names of the

mysteries. I'd already read two — *Don't Go Near the Duck Pond* and *The Secret in Locker 437* — but the others were new.

"Thanks, Gram," I said. Gram Diamond is my best supplier of mystery books, even better than the library.

"Hey!" she said. "What's the matter? You sound like you lost your best buddy."

"Well, no. Not exactly." I explained that I still had Jesse, but he and I couldn't be in *Night of the Neems*. Before she could ask what a neem was, I told her why.

"They won't let you go because *I'm* coming?"

"Er ... yes."

"Well, that's a load of horse hooey," said Gram.

I didn't answer. It *was* horse hooey.

"Listen, Stevie, I'll fix everything."

"You'll — what?"

"You need a chaperone, right? And you're supposed to spend time with your poor old Gram?"

"Uh, yes."

"Two birds with one stone, kid. *I'm* your chaperone!"

I sucked in my breath. "Gram! Do you mean it?"

"Stevie-girl, I *love* the movies. You and Jesse and I will have a fantabulous time together. It'll be a blast." She said a bunch of other things, too. Once Gram gets started, it's hard to stop her. She ended by asking to speak again to "those nervous Nellies," meaning my parents, and I knew my movie problems were practically solved.

So I stopped pacing and started my homework instead. Since I'd have to talk to Ms. Warkentin about missing school, I did a real A$^+$ job. Even my handwriting looked good.

Later, as I stood brushing my teeth, my mom poked her head into the bathroom and told me she had good news. Gram had offered to chaperone and, provided we could arrange things with my school, maybe the movie would work out after all. My mom's cheerfulness looked genuine now, and I realized that *Night of the Neems* solved a problem for her, too — how to deal with Gram Diamond's visit.

I thought about how lucky I was to have a grandmother who was "a force."

I don't know why it didn't cross my mind that "a force" is something you can't always control. You can't stop a tornado, right? You can't harness a hurricane. Throw in a major motion picture and some criminal activity, and you're bound to have trouble.

Of course, I didn't know about the criminal activity then. But I *did* know about Gram Diamond.

I should have seen it coming. The trouble, I mean.

CHAPTER

S CHOOL THE NEXT DAY LASTED AT LEAST A HUNDRED hours. But I paid extra-close attention and laughed at all Ms. Warkentin's jokes — even the math joke about rabbits and multiplication, which I didn't get. At lunchtime, my dad dropped in to talk to her. He tracked me down in the schoolyard afterward and said it was okay to miss school because there'd be a tutor on the movie set.

"A tutor? You mean, like a teacher?"

"Someone to help you keep up with your schoolwork. Ms. Warkentin's had students working on movies before. She's agreed to give you all your reading and assignments ahead of time. You won't miss a thing."

"Great." So much for a holiday from school.

After school, Jesse's mom drove Jesse and me to the T-for-Talent Agency. Before we left, I spent twenty minutes in the bathroom fixing my hair, which is kind of like taming a wild animal. I have a lot of hair — a lot! — and every strand grows exactly the way *it* wants to grow. Mostly sproinging right out from my scalp. I put some water on it and tried to flatten it, but there's not much I could do. I smiled into the mirror. Best black jeans. Last clean sweatshirt. I'd even scrubbed my running shoes with paper towels.

Jesse didn't even try. He was wearing an old faded T-shirt with a cartoon of a gorilla sticking its finger up its nose. His jeans and shoes were smeared with dried mud from playing soccer at lunch. His mom tried to brush him off, but it was hopeless.

"What's the big deal?" said Jesse. "I'm not going to wear this stuff in the movie."

I was too annoyed to answer. Maybe if I stood in *front* of him in the agent's office ...

The T-for-Talent Agency was in an old brick building, kind of run-down looking. But the office was fancy, with leather furniture and thick white carpets. The walls were covered in huge black-and-white photos of actors. I imagined my own face up there — looking back over one shoulder maybe, my eyes dark and mysterious. There were a couple of photos like that.

A tall curly-haired guy named Brad invited us into a little office. He was wearing a shiny green shirt and a tiny gold earring. Handing Jesse's mom some forms to fill out, he took my picture and then Jesse's. Then he showed us a book full of photos. Most of the kids looked ordinary, but a few were gorgeous. Unlike Jesse, they all looked *clean*.

"You could at least have combed your hair," I whispered.

"Why?" he whispered back. "You didn't."

Brad spoke to me and Jesse as if we were grown up. He said there was work coming up for child extras in the next few months, and that Jesse could start the next day on *Night of the Neems*.

It took a second for this to reach my brain. I held up one hand. "Excuse me? Did you say — Jesse?"

Brad gave an apologetic smile and shrugged. "Here's the thing, Stevie. They want eight-to-twelve-year-olds."

"I'm barely thirteen!"

"The age doesn't really matter. But you have to *look* the right age — and be the right height."

The right height? Uh-oh. I'd been doing a lot of growing lately. Somehow I'd gotten half a head taller than Jesse.

"Sorry," said Brad, closing the book.

NO! This couldn't be happening. All that planning, all that begging, all that work — to get *Jesse* in the movie?

"Listen, Mr. — uh, Brad. I'm not really this tall. I mean, I am, but I can be much shorter. See? Look!"

I slouched down onto one hip. Brad just smiled.

"Don't worry, Stevie. There'll be other chances."

I didn't hear the rest of what he said. I was too busy listening to a voice in my head that was going "AAAAAAAAAAAAAA!" It kept it going "AAAAAAAAAAAAAA!" all the way out to Mrs. Kulniki's car. I think Jesse's mom said something, but the voice drowned her out. It was now going "Rats! Rats! Rats! Rats!"

As soon as Jesse and I were in the back seat, he patted my hand. His forehead was wrinkled with sympathy.

"Sorry," he said.

"Thanks."

I spent ten seconds being glad I had such a good friend. Then I went back to the voice. "Rats! Rats! Rats! Rats!" It lasted most of the way home.

The house was empty. A note on the table said, "Gone to get Gram at airport. See you soon. Congrats on the movie! Love, Mom and Dad."

I picked up a pencil and made a thick black line through the "Cong," leaving ...

"Rats!" I said, kicking the table. "Rats on the movie!"

How was I supposed to explain this to Gram? She was almost as excited as me. It wasn't fair! How could I help how tall I'd grown? What did they have against tall people, anyway?

When the phone rang, I almost didn't answer it. Grabbing it at the last second, I grunted, "Hello?"

"Hello," said a woman's voice, uncertainly. "Mrs. Diamond?"

"No," I said, still thinking about the rats. "This is Stevie."

"Oh. Stevie. This is Melanie from T-for-Talent. When you and Jesse left, you forgot to get the directions to the movie set tomorrow. They're expecting you at 8:00 A.M."

There was a long pause as I took this in.

"Expecting *me?*" I said finally.

"You and Jesse," said Melanie. "Brad's gone for the day, but he gave me the file and said that your mom — or was it Jesse's mom? — didn't take the directions. I just called the *Neems* people and told them you're coming. Stevie Diamond and Jesse Kulniki. Is there a problem?"

"No problem," I said quickly. Inside my brain, the rats were turning into butterflies and fluttering with joy. "Where do we go?"

I wrote down the directions and said good-bye. I dialed Jesse and left a message on his machine. Then I tried to figure out what had happened. I was pretty sure Brad hadn't changed his mind, so there must have been some mix-up between him and Melanie.

I didn't care. I was in the movie! I was going to the set tomorrow! All I had to do was figure out how to get half a head shorter.

I was swooping around the kitchen, knees bent — looking *quite* short, I thought — when my parents came in. With Gram Diamond.

Throwing her arms wide open, she bent over into a crouch. "STEVIE-GIRL!" she yelled.

I ran into her arms and we swooped around the kitchen together, Gram singing ya-da-da, ya-da-da to keep us going. I got a little tangled up in her red cape, and my head kept banging against her hat — a big navy one with a wide stiff brim. Gram has a thing for hats. She has a whole closet full. Also shoes. Name a color — any color — there's a pair of shoes to match in Gram's closet. Today she was wearing ankle-high red boots — to match the cape, I guess.

"Who's going to have a *grrreat* time in the movies?" she asked and then waited, her mouth open wide in a grin, for the answer.

"Um … us, Gram," I said. I glanced over at my parents, who were standing by the door looking as if they were at the back of a theater and couldn't find seats. Gram has that effect on people.

"Hol-ly-wood, here we come," sang Gram, grabbing me again. More ya-da-da, ya-da-da. By the time we slowed down, my mom was making tea, and my dad was sitting at the table, leafing through the newspaper.

"How was the audition, Stevie?" My mom talked in that slightly nervous voice she always uses around Gram.

"It wasn't really an audition." I told them about it, leaving out the part about being too tall. Good thing Melanie and I had straightened that out.

"We'll have to be up at the crack of dawn," said Gram happily. I nodded. Gram was always up at the crack of dawn. Usually, she'd been for an hour-long walk before anyone else opened their eyes.

My dad cleared his throat and shook his newspaper. "I ... uh, hate to rain on your parade, Stevie, but there's an article here about your movie. It has me a little concerned."

Gram put her arm around Dad's shoulder and squeezed. "Oh, you!" she said, giving him a big kiss on the cheek. "You're always *concerned* about something."

My dad squirmed. Whenever Gram shows up, he starts looking about six years old. "No, really," he said, wiggling around in his seat. "Look at this."

I leaned over. The headline of a small article said IS *NIGHT OF THE NEEMS* JINXED? Right below that, it said "Trouble on Local Movie Set."

"Read it out loud, Mike," said my mom from the counter, where she was filling the sugar bowl.

So he did. The article said that *Night of the Neems* had started filming in Vancouver a few days earlier — directed by Frank Brusatti and starring Sir James Sloane.

"No!" Gram slapped both hands against her cheeks. "Really? Sir James Sloane?"

"Yes," said my dad, "but that's not the —"

"Sir James Sloane! Incredible. He's my favorite actor ever — after Mel Gibson and Harrison Ford. And Clark Gable, of course, but he's dead. Sir James Sloane!"

"Fine," said my dad, a little impatiently. "But *this* is the important part."

He read on. Accidents had been happening on the set of *Night of the Neems*. A camera had fallen over, injuring a member of the crew, and some cast members had gotten food poisoning from contaminated mushrooms at lunch.

"I don't even *like* mushrooms," I said quickly. It wasn't hard to see where this was going.

"Sir James Sloane," said Gram, staring out the window. "He was in *Tell Mary I Love Her*, wasn't he, Valerie?"

"Um, I think so." My mom let go of the tea tray a little too soon, and it hit the table with a thunk that made tea slop out of the pot. "Oops," she said.

My dad kept reading. There was more about the director, Frank Brusatti. Apparently, there'd been minor accidents and injuries on the last movie he directed, too. He was getting a new nickname around town — Bad Luck Brusatti.

"Minor accidents?" I said. "That means nothing serious, right?"

My dad raised his eyebrows. "Well, I'd call food poisoning pretty serious. Wouldn't you, Valerie?"

He gave my mom a questioning look. She bit her bottom lip. Bad sign.

"I adored *Tell Mary I Love Her*," said Gram, with a dreamy smile. "Especially the sad scene at the end when the ship went down."

"Nobody died, right?" I said, thinking about the mushrooms.

"Almost everybody died." Gram frowned. "It was the *Titanic*, for Pete's sake!"

My dad looked from me to Gram, then rolled his eyes. "I'm not sure this *Neems* thing is a good idea, Stevie. If people are getting hurt ..."

"What?" said Gram, finally paying attention.

"I said — I'm not sure Stevie should be in this movie. Food poisoning, accidents ..."

"Oh, for goodness sake, Mikey. You're not going to get into one of your flaps, are you?" Gram reached across the table and squeezed my mom's hand. "When he was little, he worried about everything. Monsters in the closet, spiders in his bed. He even worried about taking a bath. Remember, Mikey-boy? You thought you'd get sucked down the drain?"

My dad looked as though he'd like to get sucked down a drain right now — and end up in some other house. Maybe some other city.

"You kids worry too much." Gram patted my mom's hand. "Loosen up. Relax. Enjoy yourselves! I'm the chaperone, right? I'll take care of Stevie."

I glanced over at Mikey-boy — I mean, my dad.

All the fight had gone out of him. My mom just sat there, blinking.

"Well, good!" said Gram. "Stevie? Big day tomorrow. Crack of dawn! Off to bed now."

"Right," I said. Better make my getaway. "Crack of dawn."

As I reached the door, Gram's voice stopped me. "Stevie?"

I turned around. "Yeah?"

"What's a neem?"

I grinned. "Something really great, Gram."

She grinned back. "That's what I thought. See you in the morning."

CHAPTER

THE MOVIE SET WAS ON THE OUTSKIRTS OF Vancouver. It took almost an hour to drive there. Gram Diamond talked the whole way, giving us details of probably every movie she'd seen since 1952. All Jesse or I had to say was "uh-huh," and she was good for another five minutes. As we got close, she told us to watch for signs that said NEEMS. They were tacked to poles and made of white cardboard, with bright pink arrows showing where to go.

I don't know what I expected a movie set to look like. This one was a bunch of trucks and long white trailers, lined up beside a big old-fashioned building. The building was green with white trim and had three stories and dozens of windows. People and equipment were all over the front lawn.

Gram parked the car and asked a guy carrying a roll of electrical cable for directions. We made our way to a giant white tent behind the house. A table outside had a sign that said EXTRAS.

Behind the table sat a woman in her twenties. A long braided ponytail hung out the back of her black baseball cap. A couple of guys in baseball caps slouched at the edge of her table, drinking coffee. All of them wore faded jeans.

"Yes?" said the ponytail woman. She looked up from some papers she was writing on.

Gram beamed and swirled her cape over one shoulder. She was wearing a small gray hat today, with a curly red feather that swooped low and just missed her eye.

"Reporting for duty!" she boomed. "Diamond, Diamond and Kulniki. My granddaughter, Stevie here, will be performing in your movie. And this is her friend, Jesse, also an actor. I'm just the chaperone, and I'll try to stay out of your way. You won't even know I'm here. Magdalena Diamond." She snatched the ponytail woman's hand and shook it, hard.

The baseball-cap guys had gotten off the table to watch. Gram gave them a cheery wave. Bending toward the woman, she lowered her voice, which still carried at least to the parking lot. "Is Sir James here yet?"

"Uh … no," said the ponytail.

"Having a little lie-in, is he?" Gram wrinkled her nose. "Good for him. He needs his rest."

Jesse's head shrunk a little into his neck, and his neck shrunk the same distance into his sweatshirt. From the look of things, he was trying to disappear.

The ponytail woman just sat there for a moment, as if she was trying to remember what to do. Finally, she ran her finger down a list on her desk.

"Uh, Stevie Diamond and Jesse ... Kulniki, right? Yes, here you are."

Then she looked up at me and frowned. "Stevie?"

"Yes?"

"How tall are you?"

Oops. I slunk down onto one hip. "I'm not exactly sure," I said. "About average, I'd say."

Jesse's head came out of his neck. He stretched himself up straight, trying to make himself look taller — and me shorter. I don't think it made any difference, but I appreciated the thought.

"Could you come with me?" asked the ponytail woman. We all started to follow. The ponytail stopped.

"You two can go into the extras' tent," she told Gram. "Right through there." She pointed. "Stevie and I will be right back."

Before Gram could say a word, the ponytail whisked me away. As we hop-stepped across a soggy lawn to the big green building, the walkie-talkie on the back of her belt bobbed up and down. Inside, we hustled down some hallways and ended up in a small office, crowded and messy. A thin pretty woman dressed in black was sitting on the edge of a desk. Her red hair was short and spiky, and her wire-rimmed glasses were perched halfway down her nose. She was waving her hands around as she gave orders to a couple more baseball-cap people.

"Hey, Moira?" said the ponytail. "This is Stevie, one of the extras. What do you think? Too tall?"

The red-haired woman gave me the once-over. Her eyes narrowed. Uh-oh.

I pulled out every trick I knew. Slumped sideways onto one hip, bent my knees, even turned in my ankles. Reaching up, I mashed down my hair. All I needed was for my *hair* to make me taller.

The red-haired woman frowned. "Mmm ... I see what you mean."

"No," I said. "Wait. Please! I'll slouch. See? I'll bend my knees."

She didn't answer. Okay, time to beg.

"I'll do anneeeeething," I said, twisting my hands together. "Pleeeeease let me stay."

A baseball-cap woman with freckles giggled. "Aw, come on," she said to the red-haired woman. "Look at that hair!"

The redhead squinted at me. "Yes ... that hair."

The other baseball cap — a guy — let out a chuckle. "Neem hair! She has perfect neem hair."

Neem hair?

They were all chuckling now.

"Won't even need a wig," said the guy, and they laughed harder.

"Oh, Stevie, I'm sorry," said the redhead, patting me on the arm. "It's just —" She collapsed in giggles.

Okay, so I didn't know what they were laughing about. And I didn't have a clue what neem hair was. But it had turned us all into buddies, and that was a good thing, right?

"I really, really, *really* want to be in this movie," I said, "and I'm glad you like my hair."

That did it. They laughed so hard I thought they were going to hurt themselves. After the redhead finally got herself under control, she apologized again — for what, I wondered — and said, okay, they'd give me a chance. The ponytail led the way back outside.

"You're lucky," she told me. "They needed a good laugh. The way things have been going lately, we all do."

I wanted to ask why, but she was already three steps ahead.

Jesse and Gram Diamond were waiting inside the tent. So were about thirty other kids and their chaperones. They were sitting around long tables on those folding plastic chairs you see in auditoriums. Most of the kids looked younger than me and Jesse. A couple seemed to be about our age. Short, of course.

Jesse and Gram rushed over, looking worried.

"It's okay," I said. "I'm in. They're letting me stay."

"I knew it!" Gram snapped her fingers. "These people can spot talent."

As we headed for their table, Jesse whispered, "How'd you do it?"

"I have neem hair," I whispered back.

"What's —"

"Don't ask."

We sat down at a table with two girls, a boy, two moms and a dad. I glanced around the room. Were all these kids extras? Man! How was I going to get noticed in this mob?

Then I remembered. I had *already* been noticed. My neem hair made me stand out. Smiling at the memory, I fluffed my hair with my hands.

Over by the door, the woman with the ponytail was trying to get everyone's attention. "Excuse me! Listen up!" The mumbling died down.

"Hi," she said. "I'm Robin, and I'm the extras wrangler. That means I'll be organizing you guys and letting you know when they need you on set."

"Wrangler?" Jesse frowned. "Isn't that someone who herds horses?"

"Shh!" hissed a girl. Her short dark hair was perfectly cut, with a barrette holding it to one side. Definitely *not* neem hair.

"The movie we're making is called *Night of the Neems*," Robin continued. "It's a horror film set in 1919. It takes place in an orphanage full of kids." She smiled. "That's one of the reasons we need all of you."

Everyone smiled back, especially Barrette Girl.

"Here's how the story goes. Deep beneath the orphanage are some underground caverns. Living in the caverns is an evil race of small blue creatures called neems. For centuries, the neems have been searching for a route up into the world. As our movie begins, they have finally discovered a way — through the cellar of the orphanage."

Beside me, I could feel Jesse tense up. He has this problem with horror movies.

"What about the orphans?" he whispered.

"Shh!" said Barrette Girl again.

"The neems gradually take over the bodies of the orphans —"

"I knew it!" whispered Jesse.

"— and they wander through the countryside at night, creating havoc. They take over a local graveyard and attempt to waken the dead, whom they mistake for underground creatures like themselves."

"Waking the dead?" whispered Jesse. "Aw, no! I *hate* when they do that."

"Creepy," agreed Gram, her eyes gleaming with excitement.

Robin rubbed her hands together. "Well, there's more, but that will give you an idea. Some of you kids will be playing orphans, and some will be neems. There'll be special computer effects added later for the neems, but the director wants close-ups of blue creatures, and that's where you guys come in."

Wait a minute. There was something still missing here. I put up my hand. "Excuse me?"

"Yes … uh, Stevie?"

"What's a neem?"

There was a pause. Robin smiled. "I told you. Small blue creatures who live underground."

"Yeah, but what exactly are they? Like, are they mutants? Or aliens from some other planet?"

Robin held the smile. "Well, they're —"

"Monsters?" suggested Jesse.

"Well, I'm not really —"

"Prehistoric creatures?" I said.

"Spirits?" suggested Gram.

Other extras were calling out ideas. Elves, ghosts, trolls …

Robin wasn't smiling anymore. "It doesn't matter!" she said finally. Sort of yelled, actually. "They're just neems. Okay?"

Well, it wasn't okay. I still didn't know what a

neem was, let alone what kind of hair a neem had. But I figured I'd better not push my luck. The rest of Robin's talk was about how we'd have to stick around the extras' tent so we'd be there when they needed us, and we should let her know if we were going to the bathroom. She also talked about call times, which meant when we were supposed to show up, and how to behave during filming.

Then the red-haired woman, Moira, came in. Robin introduced her as one of the assistant directors. She and Robin walked around, staring at the extras and writing things down. When they got to Jesse, Moira circled around him, peering into his face and even smoothing his hair.

"Orphan," she said. "Definitely."

"And Stevie?" said Robin.

Moira smiled. "Neem." Robin smiled, too, and wrote it down.

As soon as they were gone, I started grumbling to myself. At least, I *thought* it was to myself.

"Something wrong?" asked Gram.

I knew I should be grateful for being in the movie at all. I knew I shouldn't complain, especially to Gram. But I couldn't stop myself. "Jesse gets to be an orphan. Lovable. Cute. Pathetic. And me? What am I going to be? A slimy evil *thing* that crawls out of the basement."

Gram started to answer, but I cut her off.

"I don't even know what kind of thing. *They* don't know what kind of thing. How am I supposed to act when I don't even know my role?"

"Don't forget the good part," said Jesse.

"What good part?"

"You have neem hair."

"I don't *want* neem hair!"

Barrette Girl turned and smirked. Orphan, of course.

Gram patted my hand. "Don't worry about a thing, Stevie. I'll speak to the director. Frank what's-his-name. Just you leave it to me."

Uh-oh. Gram was heading for the door. She was actually going to —

"Gram, no!" I didn't know much about movies, but I *did* know that the fastest way to get kicked off one was to have my grandma bugging the director.

"But Stevie —"

"It's okay. Forget it. Neem is fine!"

"Are you sure?"

"Gram, please. I *want* to be a neem."

After that, we all sat around on our plastic chairs in the big white tent. Someone came with coffee and orange juice and muffins, and then we sat some more. We could leave to go to the bathroom, but we had to come right back — just like school. When we met the tutors, it was even more like school. There were three of them — Mark, Cynthia and Katherine. They explained that they would work with each of us when we were free, helping with the homework our teachers had assigned. They took a few kids with them and left.

"Homework?" said Jesse. "When do we make the movie?"

I was beginning to wonder that myself. Why were they paying us to sit here?

A girl with long fair hair and a friendly face gave us a smile. She told us her name was Lauren, and she'd been an extra lots of times.

"They're setting up," she said. "They have to arrange the lights and the cameras. It takes forever. I always bring a book."

I thought about all those new mysteries Gram had brought me. Who'd ever think to bring a book to a movie?

Lauren lived just down the road, so she knew about the big green-and-white building outside. It used to be a boys' private school, she said, and it was going to be the orphanage in the movie.

"It's been empty for years. My mom figures it's cheap to rent. There's an old cemetery next door, too. They're using it for the graveyard scenes."

I looked around for Gram. She was roaming from table to table, shaking hands. "Magdalena Diamond, glad to meet you." Gram could have a good time in a traffic jam.

Finally, Robin announced it was time to get our costumes. Neems only.

The Wardrobe trailer looked like a cross between a dry-cleaning store and the world's biggest closet — rows of costumes, covered in plastic. When it was my turn, the wardrobe people made complaining noises about my height. Finally they handed me a neem costume.

Uh-oh ...

Now I *really* wanted to be an orphan.

It was a blue body suit made of some weird plastic stuff — rough and lumpy, like a skin disease, and dotted with patches of blue feathers.

At the ends of the hands were long claw things, kind of like fingers except there were only three on each hand. The feet were the same. Three-toed slippers with long claw-nails.

This was *not* what I had pictured for my first movie appearance. As I hauled on the suit, I remembered what Gertie had said — nobody starts at the top. Too bad she didn't tell me what the *bottom* looked like.

"Makeup," ordered Robin, herding us out the door.

The Makeup trailer looked like a beauty salon, with a row of chairs facing a long mirror, and jars and bottles everywhere. I sat down in front of a chubby woman with big glasses who said her name was Arlene.

"Wow," I said, staring into a mirror lit up by bulbs. "This is cool. Like a makeover in a magazine."

"It's a makeover all right," said Arlene. "Close your eyes."

When I opened them, my face was blue. Thick gobs of blue guck were plastered all over my face and neck. Arlene was smoothing it down and adding a layer of scales.

Scales! Like a lizard.

I clutched the arms of my chair. "Are you sure this is right?"

"Are you a neem?" she asked.

"Yes," I admitted.

"Then this is right."

She added a nose — a huge, gross thing that looked like a bathtub faucet. There was also a hunk of blue feathers sprouting out of my left cheek.

"Terrific," said Arlene, smiling into the mirror. "You look great. Go on over to Hair."

"Hair?"

She pointed to the other end of the trailer.

A guy named Nick was waiting in Hair. When he saw me, he grinned. "Are you Stevie?"

"Yes."

"Hey, everyone!" he said to the other Hair people. "Moira said *this* is what we're after. Right here."

They gathered around, clucking and admiring my hair. If it weren't for the faucet nose and blue scales, I might have felt pretty good.

Nick started doing stuff with sprays and gunk. When I finally got to see, I let out a squawk. It was my hair all right — but stiff, and sticking out worse than ever. And it was blue!

"You look ... amazing!" said Nick, shaking his head in awe. "Real neem."

"Er, thanks," I said, staring at the weirdo in the mirror.

I held up a three-clawed hand. The blue thing in the mirror held up a hand, too. I held up a foot. Same thing.

I was horrible! I would scare little kids. Even worse, no one would know it was me. My own mother wouldn't recognize me. As for showing off my acting ability ...

I tried to smile. The thing in the mirror did a weird twist with its lips. I sighed, and the thing's chest went up and down. This was *so* depressing.

Nick told me to wait outside. I trudged out, feeling seriously sorry for myself. More than anything, I wanted to flop down and have a good bawl. But with my face gunked up, I couldn't even do that.

So I took a deep breath and did what I usually do in rough moments. I gave myself a talking-to. For some reason, these talking-tos sound a *lot* like my old baseball coach. Tough it out, Stevie. Don't give up. Hang in there. You can do it.

There *had* to be a way to get noticed in this movie.

Even as a six-toed, faucet-nosed neem.

CHAPTER

MY ONLY CONSOLATION WAS — I WASN'T ALONE. The other neems were complaining about their noses and scales, too, except for a few who loved it, and *they* were the kind who dress up as Dracula at Halloween. Plastic fangs. Fake blood dripping down the chin. You know the type.

The good news was — I didn't have to wear a wig. All the other neems did, and the wigs were itchy.

When we were all made up, we were taken into the green-and-white building that was going to be the orphanage. The big front entry hall was a gloomy-looking place. It had a wide, curving staircase leading up to a second-floor landing. Little glass lamps with flames inside flickered against walls covered in icky wallpaper, the color of dried blood. The floors were bare polished wood.

I stood gawking with the other neems in the front doorway. The far side of the hall, by the staircase, was almost empty. But our side, close to the door, was jammed. Giant lights on stands, huge white screens, fuzzy hanging microphones and — wow, there it was! — a movie camera, with a bald cameraman sitting behind it. A crowd of baseball-cap people stood behind the camera. A few more were bustling around — measuring, fiddling, checking. Everybody seemed to have stuff hanging off their belts — gloves, hammers, wrenches, tape, walkie-talkies. The floor was junked up, too, with thick electrical cables.

As Robin herded the neems farther into the hall, I got a closer peek at the crew. There was something about them ...

Jittery glances. Knuckle biting. Lip chewing. Some people had their arms wrapped tightly around their bodies. Others shifted from foot to foot or walked in circles. Nothing obvious; but to an experienced detective like me, the clues were there. These movie people were nervous!

Was it us? The neems? Nah, couldn't be. People were staring at us, but they looked more amazed than scared. A short, stocky guy with salt-and-pepper hair and dark circles under his eyes walked over. He had a just-growing-in beard, as if he'd forgotten to shave.

"What do you think, Frank?" someone asked.

Frank! This was Frank Brusatti, the director. The guy in charge. The one who could recognize my potential! I gave him my friendliest smile. Then I remembered what a neem smile was like.

"They look good," said Frank, walking around us and staring. He nodded. "Yeah, this is going to work."

There were murmurs and a general sigh of relief, but the nervousness was still there. That's when I remembered the newspaper article about the accidents. Was that what was making the crew so jittery? They were as jumpy as fleas.

Frank gathered the neems around and told us what to do. We were supposed to run across the hall as a group, hunching our shoulders and kind of wobbling from side to side. Neems were supposed to be a little unsteady on their feet, probably from having only three toes and spending all that time underground.

"We'll rehearse first," Frank told us. "Just to make sure you've got it."

No problem. We started at the far end of the hall and, when Frank said "Okay," we all ran, wobbling and hunching, toward the camera and the crew.

"Good," said Frank. "That was good, kids." Then, craning his neck, he squinted in my direction. "There's one neem — yeah, you at the back — who's a little taller."

Ouch! Forgot. I bent my knees.

There was a pause. "Can you run like that?" asked Frank.

"Yes, sir. Absolutely."

Okay, so *you* try running with your shoulders hunched and your knees bent while wobbling from side to side. Off-balance, too, because you've only got three toes on each foot. I should have gotten an Academy Award!

My reward was — Frank didn't notice me again. When we were finished rehearsing, we filmed the scene for real. A baseball-cap guy yelled out a

whole lot of warnings first, to make sure everyone
would shut up and get ready.

"Quiet, please."

"Stand by."

"Picture's up."

"Roll sound."

Then finally, from Frank Brusatti, "Action!"

"Action!" meant we were supposed to start acting, and keep acting, until Frank yelled "Cut!" It
was pretty easy after the first few tries.

We did the scene — the crew called it a "shot"
— at least eight times. By the time we finished, my
knees ached and my leg muscles were on fire from
all that running with bent legs. Finally, we got sent
back to our chaperones.

The whole tent went silent as we filed in.

Gram peered into the face of a tall-ish neem.
"Stevie? Is that you?"

"Over here, Gram."

She still looked confused, so I took her hand and
led her to our table. Jesse gawked.

"Scary," he said, edging his chair backward.
"What happened to your nose?"

He looked different, too. He'd been dressed and
made up as an orphan while I was gone. So had
the other orphan-extras. Jesse's face was brighter
than usual, and he was wearing an old-fashioned
nightshirt, long and white, with a few holes in it, so
he'd look poor.

Some people had all the luck.

"You look terrific, Stevie-girl," said Gram, a little
too enthusiastically. "Just like that creature in the
black lagoon movie. Are you hungry? The lunches

are over there." Pointing at a table, she hurried away.

Lunch was a cardboard box containing a cheese sandwich, a banana and an oatmeal cookie. There was juice, too — orange or apple. The chaperones and orphans had already eaten, but they seemed to enjoy watching us. I have to admit it was pretty entertaining, seeing the sandwiches disappear under the nose faucets.

At the far table, a crowd of people was laughing and making noise. Gram's voice rang out above the rest.

"What's going on?" I asked Jesse. He was still keeping his distance, as if he wasn't sure it was me.

"Poker," he said.

"WHAT?"

"Your grandma's organizing a poker game."

Gram's voice carried across the room. "A royal flush! Hey, Shirl! Good going."

"Why didn't you stop her?" I hissed, leaping to my feet.

Robin-the-wrangler got there first. She started telling the card players they weren't allowed to gamble, but Gram cut her off with a laugh.

"Don't be a party pooper! It's only for pennies — and I'm losing, see? Down thirty-seven cents. Deal you in? Ernie, get Robin a chair."

It took some quick thinking and some even faster talking, but a minute later, I was walking Gram back to our table.

"Got to help my granddaughter with her acting," she told the people we passed. "Jason, I owe you nineteen cents. Mary Ann, come see me later. I'll give you that recipe for cheesecake."

Unbelievable. We'd only been here four hours, and she knew everyone.

So then I had to let her help me with my acting. Gram had some creative ideas for a neem walk, but I wasn't sure Brusatti would like them. She wanted to hear all about the filming, too, which she called "the shoot."

"That's what the professionals call it," she said. "Chuck told me."

"Chuck?" said Jesse.

"He's a grip."

"What's a grip?" I asked.

"A guy who moves things around on the set," said Gram. "Chuck's only doing this until he goes to college. He's going to be a veterinarian. His parents want him to be a dentist."

See what I mean? Unbelievable.

"Where'd you meet Chuck?"

"Out in the hall, on my way to the biffy."

What Gram *really* wanted to know, of course, was if I had seen Sir James. "Did you talk to him? What's he like?"

When I told her he hadn't shown up yet, she was disappointed. "I've got to meet Sir James soon, Stevie-girl. This shoot may not last."

"Why not?" asked Jesse.

"Chuck says every time there's an accident, there's another delay — and delays cost a fortune. This jinx business is scaring the crew, too. A couple have already left."

Jesse's eyes were huge. "Do you believe in jinxes, Mrs. Diamond? Bad luck?"

"Me?" said Gram. "Heck, no. I make my own luck. Always have. Problem is, the star of our movie *does* believe."

She whipped a magazine out of her purse. *Celebrity Spotlight*. Riffling through, she found a page with a big photo of Sir James.

"I got this from Chuck," she said. "It says right here — Sir James is very superstitious. Reads his horoscope every day. Won't walk under ladders. How long do you think he'll last with Bad Luck Brusatti? I've got to meet him soon."

She stared at the photo, eyes narrowed, lips moving. If she was in a comic book, she would have had a dream bubble over her head, full of plots and schemes.

There was nothing I could do about it, though, because a few minutes later, the extras were called back to the set. This time the orphans came, too. When we got to the hall, the extras in front started whispering and pointing.

Standing on tiptoe, I could see why. "Hey, Jesse! You know who's here?"

"Who?"

"Tarquin Forbes! Remember? He was in *One Big Happy Family*." It was one of my favorite TV comedies — about a family with nine kids.

Jesse got up on his toes, too. "Yeah! He was the kid with the square glasses."

All around us, neems and orphans were whispering the names of other TV shows he'd been in. Tarquin was about my age, but he'd been a genuine movie star for years. Moments later, the whispering brought us a new name — Selina

Gonzalez. I craned to see over the crowd.

Over by the staircase was a small thin girl with wavy black hair that grew practically to her waist. I had seen that hair before — in a movie called *Seal Island*. She was talking to Tarquin, who was dressed in a nightshirt like Jesse's.

"They're orphans," I said, noticing Selina's nightgown.

Orphans? Wait a minute. Orphans stuck together. Rats! Here was a whole new reason for not being a neem.

Sure enough, all the orphan extras were sent up the stairs to stand behind Tarquin and Selina, and all the neems had to stay at the bottom. In this scene, the neems got to run up the stairs — hunching and wobbling — while the orphans at the top squealed and looked scared, and Tarquin and Selina said things like "Get back!" and "Stop them!" As soon as the neems reached the top of the stairs, we'd go back down and do it again.

We did it four times, and every single time, Selina and Tarquin looked as scared as the first time. So did a couple of other kids who were real actors with lines to say.

Watching them made me want to do a great acting job myself. If I had to be a neem, then I wanted to be a scary one. The next time I ran up the stairs, I added some bits of my own.

"Cut!" said the director. "Who's doing that? The growling?"

A couple of neems in front of me turned around and pointed. Everyone stared.

"You!" said Frank Brusatti. "No growling."

"Yes, sir."

Rats. All that makeup, a stupid nose, and I didn't even get to growl.

Soon we were finished for the day — "wrapped" as the movie people called it. On the drive home, Gram told us way more than we wanted to know about Sir James. She chattered on about his home in London, his other home in Los Angeles, his three ex-wives, his favorite play — *Macbeth*, by Shakespeare — and his struggles as a young actor. She was especially interested in the ex-wives.

"He's single again, you know."

Jesse and I looked at each other.

"I'm single now, too," said Gram.

Jesse's mouth fell open, then widened into a grin. *His* grandma was a normal sort of grandmother. Grew flowers. Baked lemon tarts. Wore regular clothes.

"I bet he gets lonely," said Gram.

I let out a groan. Didn't I have *enough* problems?

Did I really need a grandmother who was trying to turn the star of the movie into her boyfriend?

CHAPTER

THE NEXT DAY, GRAM BROUGHT FUDGE TO THE SET. I'd seen her making it the night before and had even eaten four or five pieces, but I didn't figure things out till I spotted the box in the front seat of the car. It was gift-wrapped, with gold ribbons.

"What's that?" I asked, peering over the seat.

"Nothing," said Gram innocently, as she pulled away from the curb. "Just fudge. For that assistant director."

"Who?"

"You know. The one with the spiky red hair. I'll bring her some fudge. We'll talk a little. Maybe she'll notice you. Give you a better part."

"Gram!" I said. "You can't *bribe* people."

"Who says it's a bribe? Just a little gift for a friend."

"Friend? What are you talking about? You don't even know her name."

"Myra," said Gram. "It's Myra."

"It's *not* Myra. It's Moira."

Gram shrugged again. "Myra, Moira. I just hope she likes walnuts. Some people are allergic."

Jesse grinned. Easy for him.

Gram got back to her favorite subject — Sir James Sloane — and it lasted most of the ride. If I were a suspicious person, I'd have wondered if she was really thinking about my acting career when she made that fudge. It was going to be hard for her to meet Sir James in the extras' tent, and I think she knew that.

When we reached the movie location, I got hustled over to Wardrobe and Makeup right away. Staring at myself in the mirror, I decided that it *might* be possible to get used to the scales and feathers. But that nose? Never.

As we crowded into the entry hall of the orphanage, some of the extras started whispering. I followed the pointing fingers to ... Sir James Sloane. Wow! I can't tell you how strange it is to see a face you've known your whole life from old movies on TV. You feel like going up and saying, "Hey! How's everything?" Then you remember that *he* doesn't know *you* — especially covered in blue scales. But there he was, Sir James Sloane, deep in conversation with Frank Brusatti. Tall, with thick wavy silver hair, he had the bluest eyes I'd ever seen. Almost turquoise. He stood really straight and kept sucking his stomach in — except when he forgot, and then it kind of floofed out over his belt. For an old guy, though, he was definitely handsome. I could see why Gram liked him.

Well, sort of.

Sir James was playing the head of the orphanage. In this scene, he and a woman playing the housekeeper were supposed to rush out a door on the upstairs landing. When the housekeeper spotted the neems coming up the stairs, she'd scream. Then she'd point at the orphans, cowering in another doorway, and yell, "They're after the children!" That's when Sir James would yell "Over my dead body!", stand like a shield in front of the orphans, and holler things like "Tom, go get my sword," and "Sarah, fetch a torch from the fire!"

Everyone got in their places. Brusatti yelled, "Action!", and the neems started creeping up the stairs. It was exciting — but frustrating, too, because I didn't know what happened *next* in the story. All we did was creep. Over and over. The hard part was creeping at exactly the right speed, so we'd get to the top at the exact end of Sir James's speech. The other problem was that the actors kept messing up their lines, just like bloopers on TV.

Finally, it worked. We were creeping upstairs at exactly the right speed, and the actors were saying their lines perfectly. So it was a surprise when Frank yelled, "CUT! What's going on in that door?"

I looked where he was pointing.

One of the other neems turned to me.

"Isn't that —?"

Aw, noooooo. Gram Diamond. The third door on the landing had a window, and there she was — trying to get a look at Sir James. When she realized we were staring, she opened the door.

"Don't mind me," she yelled, giving a little wave. "I'm just on my way to the ladies' room. Carry on. You're doing great!"

She peered at the neems and squinted.

Oh no.

"Especially *you*, Stevie-girl. You're terrific!"

Actors, crew, neems … all eyes turned to *me*.

Floor, please open, I thought. Swallow me up.

It didn't.

Cheeks burning under my makeup, I slunk to the rear. It was like being in my own personal horror movie — *Return of the Force*.

Later, as Jesse and I left for lunch, Moira stopped us, and I was sure it was about Gram. But she just wanted to talk to Jesse. I made a quick getaway.

Lunch was an egg-salad sandwich, an orange and a chocolate chip cookie. I gobbled it all down, then went for a tutoring session with Katherine. We did some math and writing, and she helped me with my social-studies project. I discovered that there are two good things about tutoring. One, it doesn't last long. And two, you get the teacher all to yourself … which could also be a *bad* thing, of course.

Jesse didn't show up until the end of the day. I was starting to get worried.

"Where've you been?" I asked.

"With Moira," he said, looking dazed. "She gave me a part! In the movie. They want me to talk!"

I stared.

Jesse ran his fingers through his rumpled hair. "I was being a stand-in for Tarquin. I'm the same height and our hair's the same color, so they got me to stand in his place while they got the lights and stuff ready. But then, when Levi fell down the stairs —"

"Hold on. Who's Levi?"

"One of the actors." Jesse's words all ran together. "An orphan. He was just walking down the stairs — in the scene after lunch — and he fell. All the way to the bottom. It was horrible! He was grabbing his leg and screeching. They took him away in an ambulance. Stevie, he *broke* his leg. Maybe his wrist, too."

A chill ran through me. I'd been up and down those stairs a dozen times that day.

"So they needed an orphan to speak Levi's lines," said Jesse, "and I was there, so they asked me to do it."

He shook his head in bewilderment. "After that, Moira asked me to read some lines. She said I was good, and did I want to play Levi's role for the rest of the movie?"

I was too choked to speak.

"It's just a little role," he finished, looking around.

Silence.

"Stevie?"

"Yeah?"

"Are you upset?"

"No." Liar.

"It's not so great," he said, staring at the floor and poking his finger through one of the holes in his orphan suit.

"Did you get to hang around with the actors?" I asked. "Tarquin Forbes and Selina Gonzalez and Sir James Sloane?"

He looked up with a grin. "Yeah! Well, Tarquin and Selina, anyway. They're really nice!" Seeing the look on my face, he added, "Well ... sort of nice."

"What about a dressing room? Do you have one of those dressing rooms? In the trailers?"

There was a pause. "Uh-huh. But it's not so great."

"Does it have a bathroom?"

"Yeah."

"Does it have a comfortable place to sit?"

"Well, yeah."

"Does it have thirty other kids and their parents?"

"Uh ... no."

"Then it's better than *my* dressing room."

"Aw, Stevie. Don't be mad. It's not my fault."

True. It wasn't his fault. But what rotten luck. Second day on the movie and *Jesse* gets discovered. He'd probably get noticed by some director and get a big part on some new TV show. Every time I went to the drugstore, I'd see his face grinning out of *TV Guide*.

It was so unfair.

Back at our table, Jesse had to tell his story all over again and get congratulated practically to death. Barrette Girl was so excited, you'd think *she'd* been discovered.

"I'm not surprised," Lauren whispered. "He's awfully cute."

Jesse? Cute? He wore gorilla T-shirts. He had scabs on both elbows. When did Jesse get cute?

I flopped into a chair, waiting for the fuss to end. Gram was eager to hear all about Jesse's new dressing room, and especially how far it was from Sir James's trailer.

By the time I sat down in front of Arlene to have my makeup taken off, I was feeling as rotten as I looked. Being in the movies, I decided, was nothing but trouble. First the struggle to make myself shorter. Then the lizard makeup. And now this.

It was the last straw.

"I'm thinking of going back to school tomorrow," I told Jesse, as we walked to the car.

"WHAT? You can't! This was all your idea."

I just shrugged.

What could I say? That I was jealous? He already knew that.

Gram must have figured it out, too. She didn't say anything, but on the drive home, she turned up the radio — loud! Country music, her favorite. The singers had all lost their sweethearts and, from the sounds of their voices, gotten bad colds, too. Perfect for my miserable mood.

Jesse leaned forward and whispered something in Gram's ear as she parked the car. She nodded and headed for the house.

"Let's go." Jesse grabbed my arm.

"Where?"

"For a walk. Down to the beach."

"Uh-uh." I shrugged him off. "I'm tired and hungry and —"

"We have to talk."

"Whatever you're going to say won't work."

"Stevie, listen —"

"You listen. I've had it with bending my knees. I've had it with three-toed feet. And I've *especially* had it with babysitting my grandmother. You want to be a movie star? Go ahead. I'm going to be ..."

I kind of petered out, and Jesse leaped in. "A detective?"

"Yeah! A detective! That's what I'm *good* at."

"Well, that's what I want to talk to you about, Stevie — a crime! A case that needs solving. Will you *please* come for a walk?"

"A case?"

He nodded.

Okay, so I'm a sucker for a mystery. I argued some more, but not very hard. The next thing I knew, we were heading down the hill toward Kitsilano Beach.

It was a good idea, that walk. Once we got going, it was more like a run. After all that time in the extras' tent, it felt great to be sucking in fresh air and stretching my poor neem knees. Jesse didn't spill his news until we got to the beach. Perched on a huge log, we stared out at the water. A cool breeze blew off the ocean. I shivered.

"Levi's fall was no accident," Jesse blurted.

I shivered again, but not because of the cold. "What do you mean?"

He hunched over, hugging himself with his arms. "It happened right after lunch. We had just started filming when Levi went flying down the stairs. It *looked* like an accident, Stevie, like he just slipped. People said the stairs must have gotten slippery from all the neems running up and down them all morning."

I thought back. My neem feet had soft cloth soles. If the stairs were slippery, wouldn't I have noticed?

Jesse's mind was on the same track. "It seemed weird to me. How come none of the *neems* fell? So I checked, and guess what?"

He paused while a couple of joggers ran past.

"Only *one* step was slippery," he said. "Fifth from the top."

"Really? How do you know for sure?"

"I touched it. Smelled it, too. Fresh floor wax."

That stopped me. "What does fresh floor wax smell like?"

He gave me a puzzled look.

I shrugged. My mom and dad aren't the floor-waxing type. Or the dusting or ironing type either, come to think of it. But Jesse's mom? She does all that stuff. Yeah, I could see her waxing floors.

"Go on," I said.

"I smelled *all* the stairs, just to make sure. But only that one — the fifth from the top — smelled like wax."

I pictured him down on his hands and knees, sniffing the stairs. Jesse Kulniki, the human blood-hound.

"So that's why Levi fell? A waxed step?"

Jesse nodded. "I *tried* that step. It was like glass!"

He rummaged in his jeans pocket. "I searched around the whole area, Stevie. Look what I found in that little closet under the stairs." He whipped out one of those disposable cloths you use for washing dishes.

I shrugged. "A dishcloth?"

He shoved it against my nose. "Here. Smell."

I took a deep sniff, then coughed. "What's that?"

"Floor wax."

I took the pink cloth from him and sniffed again. Wow. This was great detective work! All *I'd* done was my homework.

"Let me get this straight," I said slowly. "You're saying that somebody used this cloth to smear wax on the stair — on purpose — so Levi would hurt himself. And then that somebody dumped the cloth in the little room?"

He nodded, his eyes eager.

I stared at the cloth. There were dark yellowy splotches on it. "Must have done it at lunchtime," I muttered, "or the neems would have been falling all morning."

Jesse nodded again. He was grinning now, like a kid who's just hit his first home run.

"But why?" I asked.

The grin faded. "That's the part I can't figure out. Why would anyone want to hurt Levi? Unless ... someone wanted to get his part."

We both let that sink in. Suddenly Jesse jerked to his feet. "Wait a minute! *I* got Levi's part."

I shook my head. "This has nothing to do with you. It started way before we came along."

"It did?"

"Of course!" Sparks flew inside my brain as Stevie-the-detective surged into action. "What about those other accidents on the set? The camera falling over? Food poisoning?"

Jesse's eyes got bigger. "The bad-luck stuff? You think it's connected?"

"Of course it is!" I almost yelled it. "But it *isn't* bad luck! And it isn't a bunch of accidents, either. This is ... sabotage."

"Yeah, right!" Jesse pounded his fist into the palm of his other hand. "Sabotage!"

There was a pause as we thought our own thoughts. Then Jesse spoke again.

"Er ... what's sabotage?"

"It's when someone tries to wreck things or mess them up. Like in this war movie I saw. A guy was sabotaging the machines in a factory because he was really on the side of the enemy."

"So who's the enemy here, Stevie?" Jesse's shoulders were jiggling with excitement.

"I don't know. But someone is deliberately causing these accidents."

Jesse was bouncing around on the log now. "But they won't get away with it, right? No way! Not with Diamond & Kulniki on the case. Boy, I can't wait to get to the set tomorrow, can you?"

I gave him a look.

He stopped bouncing. "Aw, come on, Stevie. Please? You're the one with the brilliant detective mind."

He really *did* know how to get to me. After my rotten neem day, those were exactly the words I needed to hear. He squinted, waiting. I guess I must have smiled or something, because when we stood up, we both knew I was going to do it.

Halfway home, I remembered something. "Wait a minute. How am I going to detect anything stuck in the extras' tent?"

We stood on the sidewalk, thinking.

"I bet your grandma could get you moved," said Jesse. "She's supposed to look after both of us, right?"

"Gram?" I said. "You want *Gram* to get me into your dressing room? You want her to talk to the movie people?"

Jesse winced. "It's risky, but do we have any choice?"

"None."

"We'll just have to keep an eye on her," said Jesse, as we started walking again. "Keep her — you know — under control."

"Hah!"

"No, really. We can *use* your Gram in our detecting work. You know how she talks to everyone? She could find stuff out for us. She could be, like, our secret weapon."

"Double hah!"

But the rest of the way home, he kept talking about how we could use Gram to "infiltrate" the crew. I didn't bother to argue. But I'd known Gram a lot longer than he had, and the idea of using her as a secret weapon made me nervous. You wouldn't use a sledge hammer to kill a fly, right? You wouldn't send a tiger to catch a mouse. So was it really a good idea to unleash a force like Gram on the movie crew?

Saying good-bye outside Jesse's front door, I

thought of something else. "You know that cloth, with the wax on it?"

"Yeah?"

"Keep it somewhere safe."

He grinned. "Evidence?"

I nodded.

"See?" said Jesse, triumphantly. "*Night of the Neems* needs you, Stevie. I need you, too."

I walked away feeling lighter than I had in days. It was like taking off stiff, tight party clothes and putting on comfy old jeans. This was what I was *supposed* to be doing.

"Hey, Stevie?" Jesse's voice from behind me.

I turned around. "Yeah?"

"I'm not glad there's a crime on the movie set. But I *am* glad that you and I are ... well, you know."

I was standing in the shadows. Could he see my face? Could he see how wide my grin was?

"I know," I said. "Diamond & Kulniki. We're back!"

CHAPTER

O KAY, SO MAYBE JESSE WAS RIGHT ABOUT OUR secret weapon. It took Gram exactly twenty-three minutes the next morning to move herself — and me — from the extras' tent to the "circus." That's what the trailer area was called. Gram had found that out from her new best friend, Chuck-the-grip.

"How'd you do it?" I asked Gram, glancing around Jesse's dressing room. It was a small section of a big trailer. It had a little couch, a table, a half-sized fridge, a radio and two chairs. It even had its own tiny bathroom.

"Nothing to it," said Gram. "I just talked to the movie people nicely."

Remembering the fudge, I decided to not ask any more questions. Sometimes, with Gram, it's better not to know.

The dressing room wasn't fancy, but it was ours. Best of all, we didn't have to stay there. Gram said that as long as we behaved ourselves and stayed close, Jesse and I could move around and watch what was going on.

"Bonus!" whispered Jesse. "We can start snooping."

I nodded. "Let's go."

We headed for the open area in front of the orphanage, where picnic tables and chairs were set up. A tent-type roof protected them from sun and rain. Some of the cast and crew were standing around, drinking coffee. Spotting the two child stars sitting together on canvas chairs, I nudged Jesse. "Let's start with Tarquin and Selina."

Jesse nodded. "Interview number one."

Before we could move, Selina walked over to *us*.

"Jesse! Hey! I've been looking for you."

Up close, her skin glowed a golden tan, and her dark hair shone like a shampoo ad. Perfect teeth, too. I got a good look when she grinned up at Jesse. She had to crane even higher to stare at me.

"This is Stevie," said Jesse.

"Hi," said Selina politely. "Are you …?"

"She's a neem."

Selina paused for a second, then gave me a small, sweet smile. Was I wrong, or was there some pity in there? Hard to tell with an actor.

Tarquin strolled up, looking totally ordinary. In fact, he looked a lot like Jesse, only paler. Uncombed hair, stunned early-morning face, baggy sweatshirt.

"This is Stevie," said Jesse, pointing a thumb at me. "She's a neem."

I gave him a look. Did he *have* to say that?

Tarquin stared at me curiously. I guess he'd never been this close to a neem before.

"I'm Tarquin, but everyone calls me Quin," he said finally. "Welcome to Bad Luck Brusatti's Danger Zone."

He waved in the direction of the orphanage. Baseball-cap people were carrying things in and out. The crowd hanging around outside was quiet — no joking, no smiling, no chatting. When a guy accidently knocked over a metal chair, people jumped.

"Everyone's so nervous," said Selina in a hushed voice.

"What do you expect?" said Quin. His voice went low and spooky. "We're under a curse, remember?" He wiggled his fingers at Selina.

Uh-oh. Detective alert. "Curse?" I said.

Quin gave me a long, slow stare. The dark circles under his eyes made him look older than twelve. He was about to say something, but Selina cut him off. "Don't spread rumors."

Quin nodded and clammed up.

I waited for Jesse to ask some probing detective questions — about the *curse*, for instance! But he just stared at Selina with a silly grin on his face.

"I bet you've been on lots of movie sets," he said to her finally.

"Not as many as Quin. I've only been acting for a couple of years. Quin's been in the business a lot longer."

Quin shrugged. "Since forever. You know those TV ads for Dry Baby Diapers?"

Jesse and I nodded. They always showed two babies toddling around a room, one looking miserable with a soggy diaper hanging off, and the other all perky in a Dry Baby Diaper.

"I was the original Dry Baby. My first job." Quin held his arms out straight and tottered around like a one-year-old.

Selina smiled. That was all it took. Jesse jumped into the act as the soggy baby, waddling around with his feet wide apart, letting out loud WAAAAHs of misery. Selina went into a fit of giggles.

It wasn't *that* funny.

The next thing I knew, Jesse was rolling around on the floor, wailing like a baby. I nudged him with my foot.

"Cut it out," I whispered. Crewmembers were watching.

So then he pretended to bite my ankle. That *really* got Selina going. She had to lean against me, holding on to my arm for support.

"I can't help it," she sputtered. "He's so … FUNNY!"

Funny? Jesse? Yesterday, according to Lauren, he was all-of-a-sudden cute. Now he was a professional comedian?

Was I missing something?

Selina hiccupped a couple of times and calmed down. Okay, maybe she was just tense. Sometimes tense people get hysterical.

Or maybe she needed something to eat. Yeah, sure. Even if she didn't, I did. The snack table was only a dozen steps away. I edged the four of us over.

The food was *way* better here than in the extras' area. There were chocolate croissants, raspberry muffins, cranberry scones, and four kinds of juice. There was also a tray of fresh fruit — the expensive kind. Sliced pineapple. Papaya. Strawberries.

I was loading up when Quin said, "Hey! There's that weird lady who stopped the scene the other day."

Uh-oh. Gram. She was wearing a long purple poncho and a cream-colored beret, and she was peering around as if she'd lost something.

"That's Stevie's grandma," said Jesse brightly.

There was a silence.

"What's she looking for?" asked Selina.

"Sir James."

I glared, but Jesse didn't notice.

"Stevie's grandma has a crush on Sir James!" he added. There it was again, that big dumb grin.

I made a quick decision. The next time I went *anywhere* with Jesse, I was going to bring a roll of tape — wide enough to cover his mouth and long enough to go around his head twenty or thirty times. Maybe I'd leave his nose free so he could breath.

Then again, maybe I wouldn't.

Gram spotted us and gave a little wave, but she had other things on her mind. Sir James had just walked out of the orphanage with a small group of people. Gram's eyes lit up, and her feet — in snow-white canvas sneakers — started moving in his direction.

Okay, so I'm a coward. I couldn't watch.

Grabbing my food, I led the way to a picnic

table. When we were all sitting down, I tried to get the conversation back on track. This was *supposed* to be a detective interview.

"Jesse told me about the accident yesterday," I said. "Rotten luck for Levi."

"Rotten luck for everyone," said Quin, chewing on a piece of pineapple. "The whole crew was shook up."

"You know who was *really* spooked?" Selina's voice dropped to a whisper. "Sir James. Did you see his face, Quin? When Levi fell? He looked like he was going to faint."

I remembered what Gram had read about Sir James in *Celebrity Spotlight*. "I hear he's really superstitious."

Selina nodded. "After the accident, he ran straight back to his dressing room to phone his psychic in Los Angeles."

"Psychic?" said Jesse. "What's that?"

"Sort of like a fortune-teller," said Quin. "She gives advice — like reading your horoscope in the newspaper — except that Sir James spent the whole afternoon talking to her."

"He missed his next scene," said Selina. "Frank was really upset." Glancing at Jesse and me, she explained, "When there are delays —"

Quin finished her sentence. "— it costs big bucks. They have to pay the cast and crew just to sit around. If things keep going this way, the movie's sunk."

He didn't seem very upset about this. He was one of the stars of *Night of the Neems*. Shouldn't he be worried?

The man who came running up behind him *did* look worried. He looked kind of like a movie star, too — handsome, even if he wasn't young — and wearing a fancy brown leather jacket.

"Catch you later," he said into his cell phone, then folded it up. "Tarquin! Why aren't you in Makeup? I told you to get there early, to make sure Annie does you today. That new guy's hopeless."

Quin sighed. "Dad, it doesn't matter who does my makeup. It's just —"

His dad held up a hand, palm out. "No arguments! It's the details that count. And speaking of details, are you taking your throat lozenges?"

Quin nodded and patted his jeans pocket. "My throat's okay, Dad."

"That's not what the specialist said." His dad had the phone open again and was poking buttons. "He said you could damage your vocal — Marty? Anthony Forbes here. We need to talk about the Cinestar West deal. Can you make lunch? Say, Friday?"

He was already walking away, so I didn't hear any more. But he turned back, pointed a finger and yelled, "Tarquin? Makeup. Now!"

Quin got up slowly, looking at his feet. "See you guys," he mumbled.

"Gosh," said Jesse, after he was gone. "Is Quin's dad always like that?"

"Sometimes he's worse," said Selina. "He used to be an actor himself. Now he's set on Quin becoming a big star."

I scrunched up the wrapping of my muffin and threw it in a trash can. "Quin's already a big star,

66

isn't he?"

"Not big enough for his dad." Selina stood up. "I'd better go, too."

"To Makeup?" Jesse popped up like a tissue out of a box. "I'll go with you."

I grabbed his arm as he left. "The case?" I whispered. "Detecting? Remember?"

He looked offended. "Of course, I remember. Why do you think I'm following Selina?"

Good question.

"Keep your ears open," I said, "and your mouth shut."

He gave me a thumbs-up and hurried after Selina.

That left me and the snack table. Not a bad combination, really. I tried a chocolate croissant, a slice of watermelon, and half a dozen huge fat strawberries. Then I stuffed more strawberries inside another croissant and polished that off, too.

Things were a *lot* better here than in the extras' tent.

Aside from the food, though, not much was happening. I headed back to the dressing room and got there at the same time as Gram. A plump young woman with round glasses was steering her by the elbow.

"Sir James doesn't *need* anyone to make him tea, Mrs. Diamond. *I* make him tea. That's my job. I'm his personal assistant."

"Of course," said Gram. "And you do it very well, Tracy dear. But a girl with your talents — you could be doing so much more. Do you want me to speak to Frank Brusatti?"

Tracy let go of Gram's elbow. "Frank? Well, I —"

"You could be directing. Acting. Writing the script. Tea? Pah! Anyone can make tea." Grabbing Tracy's hand, she gave it a squeeze. "What *you* need is an assistant."

Tracy took a step backward. "But I *am* the assistant."

Gram took a step forward. "So who says an assistant can't have an assistant?"

Tracy was getting the same stunned look my mom got around Gram. She shook her head as if she was clearing water out of her ears. Slowly, she shuffled away.

"Don't worry about the money!" Gram called after her. "I wouldn't expect to get paid."

Gram spotted me and beamed with delight. "Stevie! Look!"

She pointed at her feet. Her snowy white sneakers were smudged. No, wait. Something was scribbled on them in black pen. I leaned over for a closer look. On her left foot, it said, "To Magdalena Diamond." On her right foot was "Fondest wishes, James Sloane."

"Couldn't you have brought an autograph book?"

Gram snorted and headed up the trailer stairs. "Anyone can bring an autograph book. I wanted something special. Stevie-girl, he is *such* a nice man. A little shy maybe, a little quiet. But of course, he doesn't know me well ... yet."

"Yet?" I scrambled after her. "What do you mean — yet?"

But she was unpacking a cloth bag and didn't

answer. She took out three kinds of tea and an electric kettle and laid them out on a little plaid cloth on the counter. "He's British," she mumbled. "So I thought Earl Gray, English Breakfast, and Ceylon. Maybe tomorrow I'll bring Herbal Energizer. He looked a little peaky."

"But, Gram, his assistant just said —"

"Tracy?" Gram was pulling lemons and sugar out of the bag. "Nice girl, but she needs to relax. What do you think — plain digestive biscuits or chocolate covered?" She held up two packages of cookies.

"Chocolate," I said. "Gram, you can't just —"

She wasn't listening. She was staring at her shoes, a dreamy smile on her face.

"Such lovely handwriting." She glanced up, as if she was noticing me for the first time. "Stevie! What are you doing here? They're looking for you. Neems are supposed to be in Wardrobe."

I hurried over to Wardrobe and Makeup. I was the last neem, and Charlene had to do a rush job. She grumbled that she was making a mess of my face. Personally, I couldn't tell the difference.

A few minutes later, I was doing my six-toed walk toward Jesse, Selina and Quin. They looked right past me, proving once and for all that nobody would *ever* recognize me on the screen.

"Neems over here," said Robin. And there I was — back in the neem pack. Only one thing made me stand out and, as I bent my knees, I lost even that.

Brusatti explained that in this scene, the main orphans — Selina, Quin, Jesse and a couple of others — would be hiding from the neems in the little room under the staircase.

I knew what was coming next. In a movie like this, the monsters *always* discover the hiding place.

I was right! Brusatti directed the neems to creep past the little room and then suddenly stop!

"Nobody move," said Brusatti. "Except you, on the left. You can twitch."

"Me?" I said.

"Not you." He pointed at another neem. "Her!"

That neem stood up straighter. "Him!" he said, sounding annoyed.

Brusatti rolled his eyes. "Can we please get on with it?"

So we got to crouch there outside the room, listening ... *until we heard the orphans breathing*. It was great! Suddenly, one of the neems (still not me) jerked the door open. There they were — the orphans! Cowering. Quivering in terror.

Brusatti pointed his finger hard, meaning, "Rush them!"

Lurching, bobbing, making twittery neem noises, we stormed the door. The orphans screamed as loud as they could.

It was a lot of fun, but again, the problem with movie-making is that they do it in bits, all out of order. The scene ended when we rushed the tiny room, so I don't know if we mashed the orphans or ate them or took over their bodies or what.

The next scene was just neems, so all the orphans left. After a long wait, the neems got sent upstairs to the old-fashioned bedroom of the head of the orphanage. Sir James was waiting there, dressed in a white nightshirt and nightcap — looking a little silly if you asked me, with his skinny legs and knobby ankles sticking out the bottom. He was standing beside a wooden cabinet with a porcelain basin of water on top. A huge oval mirror hung on the wall behind.

"Neems, listen up!" said Brusatti. "In this shot, Sir James will be washing his face. You're going to creep up behind him. He won't see you till you reach here." He pointed at a piece of tape on the floor. "Then he'll wipe his face and spot you in the mirror!"

Excellent! I *love* it when the victim spots the monster in the mirror.

We did a rehearsal. When Sir James spotted us, he reached out to the mirror with one hand and said in a low moan, "NOOOOO!" Then he turned to face us, his eyes wild.

Brusatti looked pleased. "Great. Let's film it."

We started again, this time for real. As Sir James washed his face, we crept slowly up behind him. Then he saw us and reached for the mirror.

But before he could let out his moan ... the mirror moved! It did a tiny jolt. Then — BANG! — it dropped straight down onto the cabinet. The basin of water went flying. Right behind it came the mirror, crashing forward onto the floor, right at Sir James's feet. Shattered glass and bits of basin flew across the floorboards.

One of the neems let out a squeal. Then the whole room went dead still. Everyone gawked at Sir James, who stood stiff as a statue, staring at his feet. Frank Brusatti broke the spell. He reached out, almost in slow motion, to touch Sir James's shoulder. Sir James jumped as if he'd had an electric shock. Then he started to shake, really hard. Legs, shoulders, everything, as if he had the chills.

Frank lifted the heavy mirror off Sir James's feet. They were covered in broken glass. I was scared to look in case there was blood, but he seemed okay. A couple of crew people rushed over and picked off the glass — all in total silence, except for a couple of whimpers from Sir James. Finally Frank took him by the arm and led him gently toward the door.

The neems stepped aside to let them through. Sir James was limping. Suddenly he looked about twenty years older. I heard him say in a weak voice, like a little kid, "It's too much. It really is."

After they were gone, no one seemed to know what to do. Finally somebody called a lunch break, and people started filing out. We didn't need to be told that the fun was over. We didn't need to be told that this was bad.

Sir James was the star, he was old, and even a neem could see that he was in very rough shape.

CHAPTER

As THE OTHER NEEMS LEFT, I HUNG BACK, HOPING for a chance to investigate. I really wanted a closer look at that mirror — what was left of it. But the place was crawling with baseball-cap guys cleaning up, and they weren't about to let a kid anywhere near all that broken glass.

I headed for our trailer, hoping to catch Jesse. This time *I* had witnessed an accident — if that's what it was. It really *did* look like an accident. I'd been standing right there the whole time. No one had gone near the mirror. There was no reason for it to fall. So what happened?

Frank Brusatti popped into my mind — the way he'd looked as he led Sir James away. Brooding, worried, sad. But that was how he *always* looked. It was like the guy had a cloud over him. Was it possible that someone could actually attract bad luck? Was Brusatti really jinxed? Quin's words echoed in my mind: "We're under a curse."

What curse? What was he talking about?

And how did it fit with Jesse's discovery of the

wax-soaked cloth? That was no curse or jinx. That was a human being going into a store to buy floor wax and dishcloths.

But which human being? And why?

I shook my head, hoping to jar a few answers loose.

Nope. Nothing but questions.

Maybe Jesse would have some ideas. I ran up the trailer stairs and opened the door.

Selina looked up from the table with a start. "Stevie? Oh, hi! You scared me."

Jesse, sitting beside her, barely glanced up. He was hunched over a large sheet of paper, a bunch of colored pencils clutched in his hand. A drawing of an eagle, wings fully spread, covered a big chunk of the paper. A fat little book — I'd seen it before — lay open at his elbow. *Birds of North America*.

Ignoring me completely, he pointed at the book. "See, Selina? It's got a white head *and* a white tail. Two ways a bald eagle is different from a golden eagle."

She squinted at the illustration. "I get it. Are they the same size?"

Jesse took a deep breath and opened his mouth. Uh-oh. His eagle lecture was really long.

"There was another accident," I blurted.

They both jerked around to face me.

"Oh, no," whispered Selina. Her cheeks flushed, and her eyes filled with tears.

Jesse dropped his pencils on the table and closed the book.

"Tell," he said.

As quickly as I could, I ran through the facts.

"Gosh," said Jesse, when I'd finished. "What do you think? Was it sabotage?"

Selina whirled to face him. Pencils flew. "Sabotage?"

Her back was to me, so I shook my head, hard, at Jesse. What was he doing, giving away our suspicions to outsiders? He blinked, then got it.

"It's, er, just a word," he muttered. "I heard it somewhere. I don't even know what it means."

"Well, I do!" Selina turned to me. Angry red spots stood out on her cheeks. "Is that what you think, Stevie? That someone is *causing* these accidents? On purpose? Because that's a ... that's a terrible thing to say."

"Me?" I held up both hands. "*I* didn't say anything."

We both looked at Jesse, who suddenly got really busy picking pencils up off the floor. He put them one by one in their box.

"Anybody hungry?" I asked.

No one answered.

"I'm starving." I stood up. "I think it's lunchtime."

As we left the trailer, Jesse made a motion to me behind Selina's back — as if he was wiping sweat from his forehead. I made another motion back — as if I was pulling a zipper across my mouth. Looking embarrassed, he nodded.

The mood at lunch was gloomy. The food, on the other hand, was deluxe — as different from the extras' lunch as a giant chocolate bunny is from a stick of gum. A long table, spread with a white tablecloth, was covered in crusty rolls, fancy salads, hot vegetables and slices of cold ham and turkey. And if that wasn't enough, a barbecue in the back was turning chunks of salmon a crispy blackish red. I took a big serving of everything. If I couldn't be a movie star, at least I could *eat* like one.

Gram was sitting with Chuck-the-grip and a couple of other baseball-cap guys. As usual, she was doing most of the talking. Jesse and I gave her a wave, then sat down with Selina and Quin. Eating with them could become a habit, I figured. The other kids were younger than us and mostly stuck with their parents.

Selina started to tell Quin about the mirror, but he'd already heard. "Another nail in the coffin," he said.

"What coffin?" Jesse dug into a mound of pasta salad.

"The coffin of this movie, of course. A couple more of the crew quit today."

"No!" Selina's eyes widened.

Quin named some people I didn't know. "Spooked by the broken mirror. And they say Brusatti's going to fire Karen, the props woman."

"Props woman?" I repeated, holding my nozzle-nose out of the way of incoming salmon. "What's a prop?"

"All the *things* you see in the movie," said Selina with an anxious frown. "Candles, vases of flowers, dishes ..."

"And mirrors," finished Quin, one side of his mouth lifting in a kind of half smile. "Karen hung the mirror up."

"And Brusatti's blaming *her* for it falling?"

He shrugged. "Who else?" Again, that crooked little smile. Strange. Why wasn't he upset? Everyone else was.

Selina, on the other hand, looked miserable. She'd hardly taken any food, just some green salad and a piece of ham. She'd been pushing the same slice of cucumber around her plate since we sat down.

Quin noticed, too. "Cheer up, Selina!" He poked her with his elbow. "If *Neems* falls apart, you'll be able to do *Carrie Popper*."

Selina's face got a strange startled expression — like a deer surprised in the woods. She picked up the cucumber with her fork and chewed, really quickly.

"*Carrie Popper*?" repeated Jesse. Not because he didn't know what it was. Every kid on the planet knows about the Carrie Popper books. I'd read each book in the series three times, even though they weren't mysteries.

"*Carrie Popper*, the movie," said Quin. "Didn't Selina tell you? She was asked to star in it."

My mouth dropped open. Remembering the salmon inside, I quickly closed it. "You're kidding!" I sputtered.

"I had to turn it down." Selina's voice was so quiet you could hardly hear it. "We'd already signed the contract for *Neems*. I can't be in two places at the same time." She lifted a piece of lettuce to her mouth, then put it down again.

"You're kidding!" I said again. "You mean you're missing out on *Carrie Popper* because of *Night of the Neems*?"

"Tough," muttered Jesse.

Selina blinked a couple of times, and her eyes filled. "I wish you wouldn't talk about it. *Carrie Popper* is my favorite book in the whole world and —"

Instead of finishing, she stood up and walked away, her shoulders high and stiff.

"She could still do it," said Quin. "They cast another girl as Carrie Popper, but now they're saying she's too old. Selina could still get that part."

"If *Night of the Neems* gets shut down," said Jesse.

"Right," said Quin. There it was again — that smile. "Anyone for dessert?"

The lunch break lasted for a long time. We hung around, but nothing happened. Finally, Quin went to check. He came back with the news that Brusatti was trying to coax Sir James into finishing his scene.

"You know how breaking a mirror is supposed to give you seven years' bad luck? Well, Sir James has this idea that because it broke on his body, he's in for even more bad luck — seven times seven years, or something. He's checking with his psychic."

At two o'clock, when Sir James still hadn't come out of his trailer, the crew finally started setting up the cameras and lighting for a different scene. Jesse and the other main orphans had to scramble to learn their lines. Jesse was nervous, so I helped him practice. As he left for the set, I whispered, "Keep your ears open —"

"Mouth shut. Yeah, I know."

The neems were finished for the day, so I could

get un-neemed. I was heading for Makeup when I spotted Gram, hurrying around a corner of the building. She was carrying a large purple candle in a pottery holder, and she was moving pretty fast for an old lady.

I groaned. What now? I ran to catch up.

"Gram?"

"Stevie-girl, hi! Wasn't that a swell lunch? Don't you just love showbiz? You know, I think I could really —"

"Uh, Gram? What's the candle for?"

She looked as if she was surprised to see it. "Oh, that," she said. "It's for the massage."

I stood for a minute, wondering if I really wanted to hear the answer to my next question.

"What massage?"

"The one I'm going to give Sir James."

I was right. I didn't want to hear it.

"The poor man's in a state. If anyone ever needed a little aromatherapy and a relaxing massage, it's —"

"Wait a second." I waggled a hand in front of my face. "Aroma-what?"

She held the candle under my nose. "Smell," she said. "The soothing fragrance of lavender and gardenia. Excellent for the nerves. He'll love it. And now, if you don't mind, I'm kind of in a hurry." She was already scuttling away.

"GRAM!"

She stopped.

"You *can't* give Sir James a massage!"

She looked at me blankly for a moment, then burst into laughter. "Oh, Stevie-girl! Did you think

I meant his ... body? Oh, no no no. His head, honey! His scalp. His neck."

Well, I guess that was better.

"Cranial-sacral adjustment. I took it at night school. You just get the skull in a good solid grip. Then you pull it up and away from the vertebrae and —"

"GRAM!" She was going to pull Sir James's *skull* off his spine? Wasn't that what they did in the Middle Ages? As torture?

She peered into my face. "Stevie, are you all right? I guess I'm not a very good chaperone. Would you like me to spend more time with you? We could —"

Her eyes lit up. "Hey! I could give *you* a massage instead. Sure, why not? There'll be plenty of time later for —"

"Gram?"

"Yes?"

"It's okay. Give Sir James the massage."

I know what you're thinking. And you're right. Coward. I felt a pang of guilt. Maybe I should warn Sir James?

Well, heck, I couldn't protect the whole world from Gram, could I?

I headed for Makeup instead, and as Arlene slowly dismantled my face, I let my mind wander back to the "accidents." They didn't seem to be aimed at anyone in particular. Each accident had different victims — Levi, Sir James, the food-poisoned crewmembers. So if I was right about sabotage, then it was the *movie* that was the target. Someone wanted to stop *Neems* from being made. But why? Who would want to sabotage the movie?

The answer hit me right between the eyes. It was as plain as the nozzle-nose on my face.

Selina.

She had a lot to gain if *Neems* fell apart. She had even more to lose if it didn't. *Carrie Popper* was the chance of a lifetime. True, she was awfully young to be sabotaging a movie. But she was also really smart — and a terrific actor. It would be easy for her to seem shocked and upset when accidents happened. Those tear-filled eyes? That quivering mouth? Actors did that stuff all the time.

All through my de-neeming, I thought about it. Selina had motive, she had opportunity, and she was being *unbelievably* nice to Jesse. I was still thinking about it as I stepped inside our trailer.

"Hi, Stevie-girl." Gram was poking around in a small cupboard.

"Hi, Gram. Er … how did the massage go?"

"Not so good. Have you seen any painkillers?"

I gasped. "Painkillers?"

She let out a sigh. "It turned out he had a slipped disk in his back. I think I made it worse. He can hardly walk."

"WHAT?"

"I missed a couple of classes at night school. Maybe that's when the teacher talked about slipped disks. But if he takes a couple of days off, he'll be —"

"Gram! Do you know how much it costs the movie for Sir James to be off —"

"Sir James?" She blinked. "Who said anything about Sir James?"

"You did," I squeaked.

"Stevie, you get so confused. Sir James had such a crowd around him I couldn't get near. I gave the massage to Chuck. I wish he'd told me about his back problem, and now ..."

"Chuck." I collapsed on the couch, wondering how old you had to be to get a heart attack.

Gram bustled out just as Jesse walked in. Spotting the ice pack and painkillers, he gave me a questioning look.

"It's a long story," I said.

"Well, I've got one, too." Plunking himself at the table, he leaned forward eagerly. "I heard it from one of the cameramen. It's a real break in our case, Stevie."

I sat up straight. "I'm listening."

Jesse tapped his fingers on the table. "Did you know that Frank Brusatti isn't the *first* director of this movie?"

"Really?"

Jesse nodded. "*Night of the Neems* started off with a director named Harvey Flemm. He lives here in Vancouver, and this was his first big directing job. Before, all he did was commercials." Jesse's knuckles were hitting the table now, doing excited little raps. "So he was all excited, right? Thrilled. And he was doing a great job — at least, that's what Bob the camera guy says — but then after a week, he got fired!"

"Fired? You mean, by the producers?"

He stared at me blankly. "Producers?"

"The people who get the money to make the movie," I told him. "The producers hire the director. They can fire him, too." Our neighbor Gertie had explained this when I first started asking about movies.

"Oh," said Jesse. "Well, anyway, *somebody* fired Harvey Flemm. And boy, was Flemm mad. He said he was only fired because some important woman — yeah, a producer! — wanted to give the job to her brother. And guess who her brother is?" He waited.

"Frank Brusatti?"

"Exactly! Frank Brusatti."

"So Frank's sister got him this job?" I asked.

"Frank's sister *stole* him this job," corrected Jesse. "Stole it from Harvey Flemm."

I let out a low whistle. "Wow. I can see why Flemm would be mad."

"Not just regular mad. Mad enough to put a curse on the movie."

A curse?

"Wait a minute, Jesse. How could Flemm put on a curse? What is he, a witch?"

He shook his head impatiently. "No, of course not. It's what he said when he left. A lot of people heard him. Quin and the camera guy, Bob, and lots of other people, too."

"So what did he say?"

"Three words." Jesse paused, and then, in a slow, hushed voice, he whispered, "Kiss ... of ... death."

I swallowed hard. "Really?"

Jesse nodded. "Bob says Flemm was holding a *Neems* script at the time. He pointed at it, like a gun, and went like this." Jesse made a noise with his mouth, like a gunshot.

We let the echo roll around in our heads.

"Creepy," I said. "So *that's* what Quin meant when he said there was a curse on this movie?"

Jesse nodded.

"I guess it *could* sound like a curse ... if you're superstitious. But it could also sound like ... a threat!"

That got Jesse really excited. He started bouncing up and down, hard enough to make the walls of the trailer shake. "Yeah, a threat! Exactly what *I* thought. Wow, Stevie — we're hot! One day on the job, and we've already got our man. Harvey Flemm is sabotaging this movie."

I grabbed at a salt shaker, just before it jumped off the table. "Calm down, Jesse. You're breaking the trailer. You're right. Flemm has a reason to sabotage *Night of the Neems* —"

"Revenge," interrupted Jesse happily.

"Sure, revenge. But he's not the only one with a motive to wreck the movie."

Jesse stopped bouncing. "He's not?"

"No," I said. "What about Selina?"

If I'd said Winnie the Pooh, he couldn't have looked more confused. "Selina?"

I explained about the *Carrie Popper* movie. "She has a motive, too. See?"

With every word I said, his mouth got tighter. "No. Not Selina. No way."

I let a moment go by. Then, "Why not?"

"She's too nice."

"Nice? What's nice got to do with it? Don't you

think Blackbeard the Pirate was nice — at least to his friends? You think the Boston Strangler didn't pat puppies when he walked down the street?"

Jesse glared, his shoulders scrunched up to his ears. "Putting a girl like Selina in the same class with ... with ..."

"Okay, sorry. She's not a strangler. But she *is* an actor, Jesse. Maybe she just *acts* nice."

He shook his head furiously. "Uh-uh. No way. I know her —".

"Right," I said. "After two days."

He didn't have an answer to that, of course, so he just went into a world-class pout — eyebrows knit, chin stuck out, head hanging. Then he mumbled something.

"What?"

"I said, I know where to find Harvey Flemm."

"Yeah?" I said cautiously.

"Forget about Selina." Jesse smacked the table for emphasis. "I know where Flemm hangs out — at Calvin's Coffee Bar. The camera guy told me Harvey's there almost every evening, having meetings and stuff. We can go there tonight and ... you know ... trap him."

"Trap him? How?"

He shrugged. "We'll think of something. He's our man, Stevie."

Well, I wasn't so sure. But Harvey Flemm was worth checking out. Calvin's wasn't far from where we lived, either. We could walk there after dinner.

As for trapping Flemm, after six mysteries, I had

learned a few things about detective work. One of them was this — crooks don't trap easily. When they're cornered, they get desperate. And when they get desperate, they get dangerous.

Flemm sounded like a particularly nasty character.

Jesse and I would have to be very, very careful.

CHAPTER

I T WAS 7:52 THAT EVENING WHEN JESSE AND I WALKED
through the big red doors. Calvin's is like a lot of
coffee places in Vancouver. It has metal tables
outside for people-who-smoke and people-with-
dogs, and wooden tables inside for everyone else. It
serves fancy coffees and teas, plus salads and baked
stuff that you get at a long glass counter. But there's
one way Calvin's is different from other coffee
places — it's really *big*. It's got brick walls and
beamed ceilings high enough for birds to fly around
inside — little sparrowy birds that must have
wandered in a few generations ago. But we weren't
looking at birds today. Not even Jesse.

We stood inside the doorway, gazing at a sea of
heads, all sipping and munching and talking.
Nearly all the tables were full. At least half the
people were men.

"How are we supposed to pick out Harvey
Flemm?" I asked.

Jesse frowned. "Bob — the cameraman — told

me to look for a guy with a laptop computer, talking on a cell phone."

We scouted the room again. At least half the people were working on laptops and talking on cell phones. Calvin's is that kind of place.

"Any other clues?" I asked.

He shook his head.

We edged over to the glass counter. I could tell Jesse was feeling a little shy. So was I. Calvin's isn't really a kids' kind of place.

"Can I help you?" the serving-guy asked Jesse.

"Yeah ... uh, sure." Jesse searched the blackboard menu. "I'll have a ... a ... espresso."

I stared at Jesse. Espresso? He shrugged. The guy turned to me.

"Hot milk with honey," I said.

The guy put our drinks on a tray and rang up the bill. Man, we could have had *burgers* somewhere else at that price.

We sat down at a round wooden table. Jesse stared at the tray. "Which one's mine?"

I pointed at the tiny cup of black sludge.

His lower lip moved forward into a pout.

"Okay, okay," I said. "We'll share." Mixing the espresso and the hot milk, we managed to make two sort-of-okay drinks. Then we looked around. Laptops everywhere. Cell phones, too. Hopeless.

"Don't you know *anything* else about Flemm?" I asked Jesse. "Hair color? Height?"

He shook his head. "Sorry."

A moment later, "Well, there is one thing ... but I'm not sure it will help."

"What?"

"Bob said Flemm has one blue eye and one brown."

For a second, I just stared. Then I smacked the heel of my hand against my forehead. "For Pete's sake, Jesse."

He looked confused.

"How many people in the whole *world* have one blue eye and one brown?"

He shrugged. "Not many, I guess. But don't you have to get sort of close to see someone's eye color?"

He was right. I could see the eye color of people right beside us, but beyond that, it was hard to tell.

"Okay," I said. "We go for a walk. You take that side of the room. I'll take this side."

It wasn't as easy as I thought. I focused on the men, of course, and only the ones with laptops. But they were all looking where you'd expect them to look — at their computer screens — so I couldn't see their eyes. There was only one way.

"Hnnn-hmmm," I said, standing beside a gray-haired guy in glasses. He glanced up. Blue. I moved on.

I'd done four guys when Jesse gave me a little wave from across the room. We met back at our table.

"The one by the window," whispered Jesse. "In the orange jacket."

I glanced over. Harvey Flemm had a thin sunken face and short, dark hair dyed blond at the ends. He was hunched over his computer screen, looking so interested, you'd think he'd gotten a message from aliens.

"Okay," said Jesse eagerly. "Now what?"

"It was *your* idea to come here."

He grinned. "*You* make the plans, Stevie. That's your job. You're the brains, I'm the muscle."

"Muscle?" I stared at his skinny neck and bony shoulders.

He shifted in his chair. "Well, I *could* be … if we got attacked or something."

"We are not going to get attacked in Calvin's."

"You never know." Jesse scanned the room with a mean-eyed squint.

"Okay, fine. You're the muscle. So here's the plan. Flemm's talking on his phone now. So we go for another walk. This time we cruise — very, very casually — past his table. See if you can hear what he's saying. Take a look at his computer screen, too."

"Roger," said Jesse under his breath. "Good plan."

We sauntered toward Flemm's table, as casually as if we were taking a Sunday stroll in the park. Jesse even put his hands in his pockets and whistled, although you couldn't really hear him over the background music. When we got close, we slowed down, almost to a stop, and kind of sidled in beside Flemm, and — it was great! — Flemm was so busy with his phone call, he didn't even glance up. I held my breath and listened.

"The thing is, I've only got till the end of the month. Where am I supposed to come up with that kind of cash? This is killing me! I can't —"

That's all I heard. Because that's when Jesse *pushed* me, and I lost my balance, and my hip hit

Flemm's table, and I guess I knocked over his coffee, because suddenly there was this long, skinny steaming brown puddle running across the pile of papers beside his computer.

Flemm leaped to his feet as if he'd been scalded, which, come to think of it, maybe he had.

"Iiiiiiy!" he yelped.

"Sorry!" I yelped back, trying to grab a couple of papers that were fluttering to the floor.

Jesse had already taken three or four steps backward. "Sorry," he echoed. "Sorry."

People turned to stare. Someone handed Flemm some paper towels, and he started frantically mopping up. There was nothing for Jesse and me to do but walk — really quickly this time, not casually, no whistling — back to our table.

"You pushed me!" I hissed, when we were in our chairs.

"No!" said Jesse, panting. "I tripped! That giant at the next table stretched his legs just as I walked by. He's got size thirty-five feet! What was I supposed to do?"

My heart was hammering so hard I could hardly breath. I slunk down low in my chair. Jesse did the same.

"What's the plan now?" he whispered.

"Shhh!"

It took a few minutes for things to calm down. I snuck a peek. Harvey Flemm was on the phone again and seemed to have forgotten about us. I thought back to the bit of phone conversation I'd heard. Definitely suspicious. But something was bothering me.

"Jesse?"

"Uh-huh?"

"*How* could Flemm do it?"

"Do what?"

"Cause the accidents. He's not even there — on the set. So how could he put wax on the stairs and make the mirror crash?"

Jesse thought. "Dunno."

"Me neither." I shook my head. "You know what? This is stupid. This whole thing is a wild goose chase, a waste of —"

"Shhh," hissed Jesse. "Look who just walked in."

I glanced at the door. Holy smoke! It was Moira, the assistant director on *Neems*. She was eyeballing the room, looking for —

Yes! Harvey Flemm! She was waving. She was walking over. She was sitting down. She was ... giving him a kiss! Not just one of those cheek-kissy-things, either. This was a *real* kiss.

"Do you see that?" whispered Jesse.

"Hard to miss," I whispered back.

"Kiss of death?" he asked.

"It will be if they don't come up for air soon."

We watched, goggle-eyed, till Moira broke away. She shrugged her coat off, glanced around and —

"Duck!" Jesse dived under the table.

I was right behind him.

A couple of elves under a mushroom, that was us. Not a word, not a breath, not a twitch. Then Jesse made a face. He pointed.

A pair of feet was standing beside our table. Women's feet in black boots. A couple more feet came up to join them. Men's. White running shoes.

"Jesse? Stevie?"

Jesse winced. "Um … yeah?"

"It's Moira."

Silence. Then, "Hi, Moira," said Jesse. He winced again.

"Aren't you going to come out?"

A long silence. Then, "No."

One of the boots tapped the floor a few times. The white running shoes walked around in a little circle. The only words I caught were "knocked" and "spilled." A moment later, all four feet walked away.

"Go!" whispered Jesse.

It took us three seconds, max, to reach the door. We didn't slow down till the end of the block.

I leaned forward, hands on knees, to catch my breath. "That was bad," I said.

"Really bad," agreed Jesse.

"Not good detecting."

"Embarrassing."

It was downright humiliating. Diamond & Kulniki, professional detectives, hiding under a table like a couple of three-year-olds.

Darn. We'd never messed up *this* badly before. Well, okay. Maybe we had. But it was a long time ago.

"Did you hear what Flemm said?" I asked as we headed home. "Before I … you know … fell on him?"

"Not really," said Jesse. "Too busy tripping."

"Well, he said he was short of money. He's got till the end of the month to come up with a lot of cash. He said it was killing him."

"Really?" Jesse's eyes lit up. Suddenly he was talking machine-gun fast. "I told you, Stevie, Flemm's our guy! He lost his director job. So he's broke! So he wants the job back, right? So if he makes it look like Brusatti's got bad luck, the producers will fire Brusatti and hire *him* back. And that's how he solves his cash problem."

Everything he'd said made sense. Sure. It was possible.

Suddenly I had a brain wave of my own. "Moira," I said, half under my breath.

"Moira?"

"She's the answer to my question. Remember? How could Flemm sabotage the movie when he's not even there?"

"You mean —"

"Flemm's not on the *Neems* set, but Moira is!"

Jesse did a happy little spin around the sidewalk. "Moira! Of course. She could be his partner. Stevie, you're a genius."

Not really. But we were both thinking a *lot* better than we had in Calvin's.

"I can't wait to make a suspect list," I said.

Jesse laughed. "What's the point of a suspect list with only one suspect?"

"Three suspects."

"Three?"

"Harvey Flemm. Moira. And Selina."

He groaned. "Aww, no. You're not still picking on Selina."

I didn't answer. What was the point? First I'd say why-not-is-she-your-girlfriend. Then Jesse would say she's-not-my-girlfriend-and-anyhow-

you're-just-jealous. Then I'd say I-am-not-jealous-
and-anyhow-you're-a-skunk. And it would go from
there. Since I already knew the whole conversation, there was no point in having it.

I guess Jesse knew, too. The rest of the way
home, he just kept talking about Harvey and Moira.

But after we'd said goodnight and I was alone in
my room, I tore a sheet of paper out of my science
notebook. Moments later, it looked like this:

SUSPECT LIST
1. HARVEY FLEMM - NEEDS MONEY AND JOB
                - MADE THREAT WHEN HE LEFT MOVIE
2. MOIRA   - IN LOVE WITH HARVEY
                - HARVEY'S PARTNER IN CRIME?
3. SELINA   - WANTS TO BE IN *CARRIE POPPER*

I read it over a couple of times. Then I folded it
and slipped it into a tin box that used to hold
chocolates.

As I tucked the box under my bed, I felt a little
guilty. This was the first time I'd kept a suspect list
secret from Jesse. But what can you do when your
detecting partner has a crush on your prime
suspect?

It was up to me. Stevie Diamond, private eye,
was going to be looking very, *very* closely at Selina
Gonzalez.

CHAPTER

THERE'S NOTHING LIKE A FEW DETECTING DISASTERS to put you on the alert. The next morning, Jesse and I showed up at the set, ready for trouble. Maybe even *looking* for trouble.

It wasn't hard to find. Over in the food area, Quin's father was arguing with the catering guy. Something about "Tarquin's special dietary needs."

"I made it perfectly clear," Quin's dad said, in that I'm-really-mad-but-I-won't-yell voice that teachers sometimes use. "I gave Frank Brusatti a detailed list of Tarquin's food requirements."

The food guy shrugged. "I told you, I'm sorry."

Quin's father glared. Then he stormed away, muttering.

Quin was slouched in a canvas chair, by himself. I sat down beside him. "Do you have allergies?"

He shook his head, embarrassed. "I'll eat anything. My dad just ... you know ... does this stuff."

Jesse was listening from a distance. "I'm a vegetarian," he said. I'm not sure what *that* had to

96

do with anything, but it seemed to help. Quin gave him a smile.

Behind us, Frank Brusatti had shown up. The food guy and Quin's dad were both talking to him at the same time. Brusatti looked confused. Also sleepy.

That's when Sir James burst onto the scene. His hair was sticking up, wild and uncombed, and his purple silk bathrobe billowed out behind him like a king's cape. Tracy, his assistant, trotted behind.

"This is beyond endurance!" cried Sir James, loud enough to make Quin's dad and the food guy shut up.

Brusatti took a deep breath. "What's the problem?"

"My costume for today — the long black overcoat and top hat. It's disappeared."

"From Wardrobe?" Brusatti frowned.

Sir James shook his head impatiently. "Of course not! Tracy brought it to my dressing room yesterday, before we left. You know I like to rehearse my lines in costume."

"It's true, he does," agreed Tracy. "I put the hat and coat in the closet last night. I locked the trailer door, too. I'm sure I did!"

Sir James pulled his dressing gown tight around his chest. His chin was trembling so hard, he could barely speak. "I don't see how .... I can't ... impossible."

Without the costume, they couldn't do the morning's scene. Another delay.

"What do you think?" whispered Jesse. "More sabotage?"

"Could be," I whispered back.

"Keep your eye on Moira."

"Right," I said, adding to myself, "and Selina."

The crew started setting up a new scene that just needed orphans. It took a while to get organized because the main orphans hadn't learned their lines yet. Jesse only had two lines, but he was really nervous.

Finally, everything was ready. We were in a dormitory room full of metal bunk beds. I found a place to stand, behind the camera and crew, and watched as the orphans climbed into their bunks. Without my costume, I felt almost like one of the crew, especially when Chuck popped his baseball cap on my head.

Brusatti explained the scene. The orphans were supposed to be waking up after their first "night of the neems." Some of the orphans had heard the neems creeping around and were scared. Others had slept through everything and wouldn't believe the scared orphans. Jesse was a slept-through-everything orphan. His bunk was below Quin's, and he was supposed to look up at Quin and say, "That's balderdash, Bartholomew. Don't talk rot!"

As he climbed into his bunk, I could see his lips moving. I'd helped him practice, but those lines were real tongue twisters. "Balderdash, Bartholomew" got him nearly every time, and "Don't talk rot" kept coming out as, "Don't talk wot." Who wrote this thing?

He'd only been in his bunk a minute when he climbed out again, his face red. After whispering something to Frank Brusatti, he scurried away — to the bathroom, I figured. All that practicing must have made him nervous. It was okay, though, because they were still rehearsing Quin's speech — a long one. He said most of it lying on his side on the top bunk. Right in the middle, he was supposed to sit up and yell, "I *did* see them. I did, too!"

Everything was fine until Quin jumped to a sitting position. He shook a fist and yelled, "I *did* see —"

Then, "AAAIIIIIEEE!"

The top bunk collapsed!

Springs, mattress and all — it dropped straight through the frame onto the bunk below. Quin fell, too, flopping like a rag doll. His head hit the wall with a thunk just before his body crash-landed on the collapsed mattress. The frame shook and swayed, but somehow the metal posts stayed up.

Nobody moved. Quin lay there like a broken puppet.

Then he let out a whimper.

Like a swarm of bees, people raced to the bed. As Quin tried to sit up, he was grabbed by at least six pairs of hands. His dad was fighting his way through the crowd, half-hysterical. I got an elbow in my side as he pushed through.

"Tarquin! Are you — let me — get out of my way! Tarquin! Are you all right?"

I couldn't see Quin any more, not with all those people around him. But I heard his voice. "Dad, I'm fine."

Finally, the crowd parted, and Quin stepped through, with his dad hovering on one side and Brusatti on the other.

"Take a break," Brusatti barked, glancing around.

People backed off, but not too far. Everyone was watching Quin as he tested his arms and legs to make sure nothing was broken. No blood.

He walked away slowly, but without help.

After he was gone, the crew started to wander off. I felt a tap on my shoulder. Jesse was standing there, his face as white as paper. Even under that loose nightshirt, I could see his shoulders trembling. He opened his mouth, but nothing came out. Then, like a robot, he pointed at the broken bed. Stepping closer, he touched the edge of a pillow, squashed and torn beneath the collapsed upper bunk.

Then I understood. That was *his* pillow. The one his head would have been on, if he hadn't gone to the bathroom. The heavy frame had crushed it pancake-flat.

"I'm scared," said Jesse, in a voice he probably hadn't used since he was three.

CHAPTER

J ESSE STARED, AS IF HE WERE HYPNOTIZED, AT THE crushed pillow.

"I could have been —"

"Don't think about it," I said.

Easy for me. He kept staring.

I pulled him around to face me. "Concentrate on the case. Help me figure it out."

He swallowed, then gave me a slow-motion nod. His eyes looked way too big for his face.

I glanced around. Except for a guy fiddling with electrical cables in a corner, we were alone.

"Let's check the bed," I said, under my breath.

We zeroed right in on the frame — especially the tops of the steel posts, where the bunk had broken loose. The posts were shaped like corners, and each of them had two empty holes at the top. When we checked the next bed to compare, we saw right away what was supposed to be *in* the holes.

"Bolts," said Jesse quietly, pointing at the rusted bolts holding the bunk in place. "Eight of them."

"So where are the bolts from the broken bed?"

After a few minutes of hands-and-knees searching, we found seven. Four were under the bed, two more were over by the wall, and another had rolled three beds over.

Jesse rubbed one between his fingers. The rust left a powdery orange stain.

"These beds are really old." I grabbed a bed frame and gave it a shake. It rattled, even swayed a little.

Jesse frowned. "So maybe it really *was* an accident?"

Before I could answer, the guy with the cables yelled "Hey! What are you kids doing?" He must have heard the bed shake.

"Nothing," I called. "Just leaving."

Motioning to Jesse, I headed for the door. Outside, I opened my hand and pointed at one of the bolts I was holding. "See those marks?"

Along two sides, there were small scratches in the rust.

Jesse stared. "So?"

"Ever used a wrench?"

His eyes bugged out. "You mean — someone *undid* the bolts?"

"Probably loosened them just enough so that when Quin started jumping up and down, the top bunk would fall."

Jesse turned pale. I had a good idea of what he was seeing in his head. It wasn't pretty.

"If I hadn't gone to the bathroom —"

"Don't!" I said. Jesse's a worrier. Practically a professional. If he got going on what *might* have happened, we'd be back in Ms. Warkentin's class before lunchtime.

"Think," I said. "Who had the chance to loosen the bolts?"

Slowly he opened his eyes. "Everyone. The whole cast and crew."

True. I had personally seen two of our prime suspects lurking near the scene of the "accident." Selina and Moira. But fifteen or twenty other people were hanging around there, too.

"Let's forget the bed for now," I said. "What about the theft this morning? Sir James's costume. That's what started the trouble. There's got to be a connection."

Jesse looked relieved. "The costume was locked in his dressing room. Tracy said so." He thought for a moment. Then, "Why don't we question Tracy? See if she noticed anything ... you know ... suspicious."

I nodded. "She's probably in Sir James's dressing room."

Jesse led the way. I guess I expected Tracy to be sitting outside, like a secretary, keeping people out. But we couldn't see her, and the trailer door was open. We tiptoed up the stairs and rapped on it.

"Yes?" said a male voice. Sir James peered out at us, his eyes sparkly behind a pair of silver-rimmed glasses.

"We're, um ..." I stopped, not sure what came next.

To my surprise, he smiled. "Come along in. It's quite all right. Just let me find my pen."

He gestured toward a wine-colored couch

covered in newspapers. Pushing the papers aside, I plunked myself down and pulled Jesse beside me. No sense wasting an opportunity to question a witness, even if it wasn't the one we'd planned on.

Sir James's trailer was a lot bigger than ours. It had at least two rooms, and the furniture was much fancier. Two bouquets of fresh flowers stood on a counter. Other than that, though, the place was a mess. Clothes, books and papers were scattered in piles. I felt right at home.

Sir James searched the table — a jar of olives, a copy of *Celebrity Spotlight*, a Sherlock Holmes pipe, and a half-eaten box of Belgian chocolates that I wouldn't have minded trying. He picked a black-and-gold pen out of the pile. "Did you bring your autograph books?"

"Er ... no." Jesse squirmed in confusion.

"We forgot." I elbowed Jesse in the ribs. "Could you just autograph a piece of paper? Write 'To my biggest fan, Stevie Diamond.'"

Sir James dug through the mess again, looking for blank paper. "My biggest fan, you say? Well, it's certainly a pleasure to meet my biggest fan."

So then, of course, Jesse had to have *his* autograph made out "To my biggest fan, Jesse Kulniki." That bugged me — Sir James couldn't have more than one biggest fan. Then I remembered that I wasn't really a fan at all. If Sir James *did* have a biggest fan, it would have to be Gram.

We thanked Sir James, and then it was time for some serious snooping.

"Did you ... er, find your coat?" I asked.

"My coat?" Sir James frowned. "Oh, you mean my costume. No, not a trace."

"Does anyone have a key to your dressing room?" I asked. "Besides you?"

Sir James looked surprised. "My assistant, Tracy."

"What about visitors?" asked Jesse, leaping in, just a little too loud. "Do you get many visitors here?"

Sir James looked even more surprised, but still friendly. "What curious questions you children ask. Hmmm ... visitors. Yes, certainly. People stop by all the time. Dreadful to be stuck off on one's own, treated like royalty."

"Any *particular* visitors in the last day or so?" I asked.

The interview got trickier here. I could see that Sir James wasn't particularly interested in listing his visitors for a couple of autograph-hunting kids. It's times like this that I really envy the police. They can ask anything they want, straight out. People have to answer. It's a *lot* harder to be a private eye — especially a kid private eye.

In the end, by asking some sneaky roundabout questions, we found out that Moira had visited Sir James's dressing room. Selina had come by, too, bringing Quin. There were other visitors, but no one important. We were no further ahead.

Sir James stood and rubbed his hands together. "Well, this has been delightful, but if you don't mind ..."

Jesse got to his feet, and I followed. Just then, I spotted a thin book lying face down at the edge of the table.

"Hey!" I said, picking it up. *"Macbeth*, right? By Shakespeare? My Gra — someone told me it was your favorite play."

Sir James shivered as if a cold draft had come in. He put a finger over his lips. "Please! Call it 'The Scottish Play.' It's terribly bad luck for an actor to speak the name of … that play."

"Oh." I handed him the book. "Sorry."

"An innocent mistake." He turned it over, fondly. "And yes, it is my favorite. Reading it soothes my nerves."

Hah! Sir James didn't need Gram's aromatherapy or massages or Relaxing Herbal tea. He had *Mac* … The Scottish Play.

Was it bad luck, I wondered, even to *think* the title? Or did you actually have to say it out loud? Suddenly I remembered Sir James's bad luck the day before.

"How's your foot?"

"My foot?"

"You were limping yesterday … after the mirror fell on it."

"Ah, yes. The mirror. Terrible, terrible. It would never have happened if Frank hadn't allowed the children to play with the props."

"Excuse me?" I said. "Children? Props?"

"The mirror," said Sir James, sounding tired. "I quite understand that Selina needs one for her ballet exercises, but that particular mirror was fragile and had delicate fastenings and —"

I held up a hand. "Wait a minute. Are you saying that Selina was using that mirror for ballet practice?"

He nodded. "She took it several times. Moved it off to other rooms to —"

"SHE'S INNOCENT!" blurted Jesse.

"She's a dear, sweet girl," said Sir James, "and of course she didn't do anything deliberately, but —"

"Innocent!" repeated Jesse, not quite so loud, maybe because I was giving him a look-that-could-curdle-milk.

"You're probably right," mumbled Sir James. "It's the psychic vibrations on this set. Every day, some new manifestation ..." He waved a hand around at his dressing room as if he expected a ghost or a witch to appear.

"Innocent," muttered Jesse. For the third time, in case you're counting.

Sir James barely noticed. "Familiar objects disappearing, ominous strangers appearing out of nowhere ..." He paused. Just when it was getting interesting.

"Strangers?" I prompted.

Leaning forward, Sir James whispered, "There's a very peculiar woman wandering around the set. She brews odd potions and goes about carrying strange-smelling candles. She wears the most extraordinary hats, too, and —"

"Hey!" Jesse interrupted, a huge grin on his face. "I know who that is! That's Stevie's —"

A hand across his mouth stopped him. Mine.

"Who?" said Sir James.

"Nobody," I said. "We have to go now. Come on, Jesse."

I pushed him out the door ahead of me.

"Ow." Jesse rubbed his mouth. "What's your problem, Stevie?"

"My problem is my so-called *partner,* who keeps —"

I stopped. Standing at the bottom of the stairs, hands in the pockets of his jeans, was Quin. How long had he been standing there?

"Quin, hi!" I glanced back. The dressing room door had been open the whole time. How much had he heard?

"Are you okay?" asked Jesse. "That was a really bad fall."

Quin shrugged the question away. "I just dropped onto a mattress. Didn't even get a bruise."

"Still ..." Jesse looked concerned, and I could see why. For one thing, Quin had changed into his regular clothes. For another, he was hopping from one foot to the other in a kind of nervous dance. And why was he standing out here, alone?

"So what's up?" I asked.

He just kicked at the metal stairs. Hard. The banging brought Sir James to the door of his trailer.

"Sorry." Quin backed away. Sir James gave him an annoyed look and closed the door.

"How come you're not in costume?" asked Jesse. "They didn't .... uh, fire you, did they?"

Silly question. Why would they fire Quin for falling?

"... wish they would," mumbled Quin, his shoulders hunched, his eyes searching the ground for something else to kick.

"Are you okay?" I asked.

"Sure," he snapped. "I'm a big star, didn't you

know? Why wouldn't I be okay?" I guess he noticed the surprise on our faces. "Oh, look, I'm — I'll see you guys later."

He disappeared around a trailer.

"What was that all about?" asked Jesse.

I shrugged. Things were getting weirder by the minute.

Back in the food area, the first person we saw was Selina. When she spotted us, she ran right over. Jesse puffed up as if someone had blown air into him. I swear he got taller.

"Have you seen Quin?" she asked.

Jesse pointed toward the trailers. "Is something wrong?"

She nodded, twisting a strand of her long hair between her fingers. "It's his dad. He made a huge fuss about Quin's accident this morning. He threatened to sue Frank Brusatti. Kept screaming he'd shut the whole movie down."

"Wow." Jesse's voice was hushed. No wonder Quin had been upset. Most parents are embarrassing in one way or another, but this was over the top.

"Quin ran off," said Selina. "He has a hard time with his dad. Well ... with the whole movie thing, I guess."

"Really?" I said.

She sighed. "Quin *hates* being an actor. Always has. He's been in movies since he could crawl, and all he ever wanted was to be a regular kid. You know ... homework, summer camp, Little League."

"You're kidding," I said. As a regular kid, I could have told him it's not that exciting. Most regular kids would give a year out of their lives to be Quin.

Jesse looked at Selina shyly. "Is that how *you* feel?"

A smile lit up her face, bright as a spotlight, and I suddenly realized how she'd gotten so far, so fast. "I love it! I've been dreaming of this ever since I can remember."

Then she added, "But I chose this. I *wanted* to be an actor. Quin never had a choice. His dad's been pushing him since he was a baby — and now he's pushing Quin's younger brother and sister, too. Megan, his sister, is the new Dry Baby."

"Gee," I said. "What about Quin's mom?"

"I don't think she likes all this stuff. But Quin's dad ..."

She didn't need to finish. We had all seen how hard it would be to argue with Quin's dad. My parents bossed me around a lot — or tried to. But compared to Quin's dad, they were Mr. and Mrs. Softie.

"I'd better find Quin," said Selina. "See you." She walked off toward the trailers.

I nudged Jesse. "We have to talk."

The trouble with a movie set is — everywhere you look, there are baseball-cap people.

Jesse crooked his finger. "Follow me."

He led the way into the orphanage and to the big staircase — the one Levi had tumbled down. Underneath was the small room where the orphans had hidden from us neems. I followed Jesse inside.

"Dark in here," I said, once he'd closed the door. "Do you suppose there are spiders?"

"Cut it out, Stevie, or I'm out of here."

"Sorry," I said. Jesse has phobias. Besides spiders, he's scared of heights, small spaces, the dark, fast cars … you get the picture. It makes him easy to tease.

But we had better things to talk about — like the exciting new clue we'd picked up in Sir James's dressing room.

"Did you *hear* what Sir James said about the mirror?" I asked. "Selina used it to practice her ballet!"

"So what?" Even in the dark, I could sense Jesse's grumpy frown.

"Come on," I said. "She's a suspect! *Carrie Popper* is a great reason to sabotage the movie. And she had the best opportunity of anyone to fool with the mirror."

"Fool with the mirror? You think Selina would *do* that? Hurt an old man like Sir James?"

"You hardly know her," I reminded him.

"I know she's really nice."

"She's an actor. She can *act* nice."

"Hmmph!"

I wasn't getting anywhere with this. "What about Quin?" I said into the dark.

"What about him?"

I sighed. "He wants the movie to fail, too. He doesn't want to be in *any* movie."

There was a pause. "I guess …" said Jesse. He didn't sound convinced.

"Quin's really unhappy," I said.

"Unhappy enough to make his own bunk bed collapse?"

"*He* didn't get hurt," I pointed out. Jesse and I were probably thinking the same thing. The person who *should* have gotten hurt was Jesse. It was hard to believe that Selina or Quin would do that. It was hard to believe *anybody* would do that.

On the other hand, both Selina and Quin were desperate.

"Quin's miserable," I said. "He's falling apart."

"Yeah," said Jesse, slowly. "We'll have to put him on our suspect list. But not Selina."

"For crying out loud, Jesse. Be reasonable!"

"*You* be reasonable. There are other suspects out there that you're not even mentioning."

"Like who?"

There was a pause. "Well, what about … Sir James?"

"Sir James? What's suspicious about him?"

"He's weird," muttered Jesse. "All that stuff about psychic vibrations. Gives me the creeps."

A bunch of arguments jumped into my head — being "weird" doesn't make someone a suspect; Sir James had no reason to sabotage the movie; and, besides, he was one of the victims. But I kept my mouth shut. Jesse and I have been partners for a long time. I knew when to give in.

"Okay, we'll put Sir James on the list. Anyone else?"

"Quin's father," said Jesse quickly.

This was a surprise. "Why?"

"He's weird."

Right. Weird.

"I'll make you a deal," I said. "I'll trade you Sir James and Quin's father for Selina. They *all* go on the suspect list." I didn't bother telling him that the list already existed. Or that Selina was already on it.

There was a long pause.

"Okay," said Jesse, finally. "Just as long as you know, I don't believe it about Selina."

"Yeah, I know."

He coughed — a short, cut-off little sound.

"Getting a cold?" I asked.

"No. Are you?"

He coughed again.

"*You're* the one who's coughing," I said.

Another cough.

"Stevie?"

"Yeah?"

"I'm not coughing." Jesse's voice had a quiver in it.

The cough was coming from *behind* us.

CHAPTER

"AAAAAAAAAAIIIIII!!!"

Jesse and I launched ourselves at the door. There was a bit of confusion — and a lot of yelling — as Jesse tried to pull the door instead of pushing. Finally, we stumbled out into the hall, blinking in the light.

Jesse clutched my arm. "Who coughed?"

"Don't know," I panted.

We looked back at the half-open door. I tiptoed over and gave it a gentle kick, easing it open all the way. We peered inside. Dark.

"Come on out," I yelled, taking a step backward.

There was a shuffling sound. Quin crept out, his head hanging, his face red and tight. Was he angry? Upset? Embarrassed?

Or maybe just trying not to cough again?

"Quin —" said Jesse, taking a step toward him.

Quin took off at a run.

"He heard everything," said Jesse.

"I know." I couldn't believe it. We had actually discussed our suspect list *in front* of one of our

suspects. Diamond & Kulniki had blown it —
again!

Jesse shook his head. "Geez, Stevie, do you think
we're losing our touch?"

"I think we're losing our marbles," I muttered.
"We should have checked that room out."

"Who'd ever expect a movie star to be hiding
under the stairs?"

"He was an *upset* movie star. He must have
wanted to be alone."

Jesse smacked himself in the forehead. "Stupid,
stupid, stupid ..."

There was nothing to do except be glad there
wasn't any official world organization of kid detectives. If there was, we would have been voted out.

We didn't see Quin again until lunchtime. Jesse
and I were sitting at a table alone when Selina and
Quin walked in together. Without even looking our
way, they sat at a table with some younger kids.

Jesse watched Selina nervously. "Do you think
Quin told her? About what he heard?"

"She doesn't look very friendly," I said.

Jesse's face crumpled. "Oh, man ... I hate this."

So did I. But there wasn't much we could do.
After a while, Gram came along with Chuck and a
couple of baseball caps named Duncan and Joel.
To take our minds off things, I asked Duncan about
his walkie-talkie. He showed us how you hold a
button down to speak into it. Everyone else
carrying walkie-talkies can hear you — as long as
they have their sets turned on. We listened to a
couple of messages, but they were full of pops and
hisses and weren't very interesting.

After lunch, I got into my costume and makeup for another neems scene. This time, we were on the basement stairs. Because of Levi's fall, the crew had covered the steps with non-slippery rubber carpet. All we had to do was stand on them, waiting. When Frank yelled action, we ran upstairs and burst through the door at the top. The camera filmed us charging out onto the main floor.

Nothing to it — for most neems. But being a taller-than-normal neem was getting to me. By the end of the afternoon, my knees ached, and the crick in my neck was feeling permanent. We had to do the scene nine times to get it right, and I wasn't in a neem mood.

Later, as we headed for the car, I asked Jesse if he'd seen Quin and Selina.

He shook his head. "I think they're avoiding us."

I nodded. No surprise there.

No surprise either that Gram did most of the talking on the way home. "We're going to start late tomorrow," she said. "A night scene in the cemetery. Won't that be fun?"

"Fun?" said Jesse. "A cemetery?"

"Well, maybe not fun," corrected Gram. "But very romantic. Alone together in the dark …"

I figured "alone together" meant her and Sir James. She was probably picturing the two of them snuggled behind a tombstone. Sometimes I was glad I couldn't see inside Gram's brain.

Thinking about Gram's brain made me think about the saboteur. Too bad I couldn't see inside *his* brain. Too bad I couldn't see what he — or she — was planning to do next.

116

And that's when something happened in *my* brain.

About time, too.

"Are they filming in the cemetery for just one night?" I asked Gram. "Or a whole bunch of nights?"

"Just one," said Gram, checking her lipstick in the rearview mirror. "The next night, we're back at the orphanage. Filming in the basement and the yard just outside."

I leaned over and whispered in Jesse's ear. "Meet me after dinner. I've got an idea."

"Roger."

Unfortunately, Jesse's mom decided they were going *out* for dinner. That's another problem with being a kid detective — at any moment, your parents can mess up your whole investigation. I waited up for Jesse till eleven, then went to bed.

At nine o'clock sharp the next morning, I was knocking at his front door with the suspect list. With new bits added, it looked like this:

SUSPECT LIST

1. HARVEY FLEMM — NEEDS MONEY AND JOB
   — MADE THREAT WHEN HE LEFT

2. MOIRA — IN LOVE WITH HARVEY
   — HARVEY'S PARTNER IN CRIME?

3. SELINA — WANTS TO BE IN *CARRIE POPPER*
   — HAD A CHANCE TO MESS WITH MIRROR

4. QUIN — WANTS TO GET OUT OF ACTING

5. SIR JAMES — WEIRD

6. QUIN'S FATHER — WEIRD

Jesse came to the door in lime-green pajamas covered with tiny red-nosed reindeer — Christmas jammies. I've got a few of those, too, stuffed in the back of my cupboard.

"Come on in," he said. "My mom's gone to work."

I followed him into the kitchen. His breakfast was on the table. Raisin toast and peanut butter. I handed him the list, and he did a quick read while I stuck more bread in the toaster.

"That's a lot of suspects," he said.

"Yeah," I agreed. Personally I wasn't taking the last two names very seriously. "Want to make any changes?"

"Uh ... no." He was dying to snatch up a pen and cross out Selina's name. "So what's your idea?"

I buttered my toast and grinned. "I think we've been doing this backward."

"Backward?"

"Yeah. We keep waiting around for the saboteur to do something. Wax the stairs. Mess with the mirror. Loosen the bolts on the bed. Then we try to figure it out. We're following the saboteur."

Jesse took a sip of orange juice. "So?"

"So how about we get *ahead* of him?"

"Ahead?" He frowned. "I don't get it."

"We *guess* where the saboteur is going to be next. We get there first and wait for him or her to show up."

"Like an ambush!" said Jesse, his face lighting up.

"Exactly!" I took a bite of toast.

"Good one, Stevie."

"We start tonight," I told him. "The crew will be filming in the cemetery. If something's going to happen there tonight, we're too late to do anything except stand around and watch. We have to think about *tomorrow* night."

Jesse was on his feet, pacing the kitchen floor. "Yeah. Cool!"

"Tomorrow we'll be filming in the basement of the orphanage. If I'm right, the saboteur will be in the basement *tonight*, setting up something to go wrong on tomorrow's shoot. And that means that you and I —"

Jesse stopped in his tracks. "I'm beginning to get a bad feeling about this."

"— will get there first. We'll sneak into the orphanage tonight, hide in the basement, and wait."

There was a pause. "I don't know, Stevie. Are you sure this is a good idea? To be in the basement? Alone? At night? With ... him?"

"It's a simple little stakeout," I said, dusting crumbs off my shirt. "All we're doing is spying, to see who shows up."

Another pause, longer this time. "What if they need us for the movie?"

"Don't worry. Gram said tonight is mostly neems running through the cemetery."

Actually, I *was* a teensy bit worried. What if the neems got called and I wasn't around? Still, it wasn't as if I had an important part. They might not even notice I was gone.

We spent the rest of the day on schoolwork.

"I can't believe that tutor," muttered Jesse. "Eleven little spelling mistakes, and she gets all choked up."

I grunted in sympathy. Homework — in the middle of a mystery. This *never* happens to adult detectives.

You think Sherlock Holmes worried about spelling? Hah!

Gram was dressed all in black as we left the house that evening. Good for snuggling behind tombstones, I guess. Her hat was a kind of cowboy thing, decorated with a bucking bronco pin, and her long black cape wound around her like a blanket. She hummed happily to herself as she drove.

It was getting dark when we arrived. Good. The makeup call for neems was delayed. Very good. We headed for the cemetery where the crew was busy setting up equipment — there were *lots* of lights — and everyone else was just hanging around. The snack table was set up in a corner of the cemetery, under an awning.

After ten minutes or so, I took a good look around. Everyone was busy, including Gram, who had gotten into a conversation with Tracy. A typical Gram conversation — Tracy was doing all the listening.

"It's time," I whispered to Jesse.

He nodded, and we shuffled slowly toward the cemetery gate. Every now and then we glanced around to see if anyone was watching.

At the gate, we broke into a run. We raced down the street to a gravel driveway that wound, through some bushes and trees, to the rear of the orphanage. It loomed high above us, a black outline against the darkening sky. No lights on inside. No lights outside either, except for the trailers in the distance. I squinted at the fire escape — a metal stairway attached to the back of the building. I'd seen some of the little kids playing on it until a baseball-cap guy told them to get off. It climbed to some landings on the second and third floors where there were doors and windows. I was counting on one of them being unlocked.

"Let's go," I whispered to Jesse.

After a couple of steps, he grabbed my arm.

"Where are you going? It's over there." He pointed to a door at ground level.

"It'll be locked," I said. "We'll take the fire escape."

"WHAT?" Jesse's voice was suddenly louder. Higher, too. "That rickety old thing?"

Uh-oh.

"No way," he said. "Forget it, Stevie. Not in a million years. Not in a trillion GAZILLION years!"

That sounded pretty definite.

"I'll go first," I offered.

"Sure. You go first. I'll follow you. In three DAYS!"

For a minute or so, we didn't speak. The air buzzed with grouchy thoughts.

Time to get serious.

"Jesse?"

"Yeah?"

"Do you want to solve this mystery?"

"Well, yeah, but —"

"Do you want to stop these accidents?"

"Of course, I —"

"So how do you plan to do that? At home in your reindeer pajamas?"

Before he could answer, I gave him the kind of lines that always work in movies. "We're in this up to our necks, Jesse. There's no turning back. We're in too deep. It's do or die. The only way out is —"

"All right, all right already. Can we at least *try* the door first?"

I followed him to the back door.

"Stevie?"

"Yeah?"

"Those pajamas ..."

"Yeah?"

"My Aunt Ellie in Toronto ..."

"Sure, Jesse. I know you didn't pick them."

"No way!"

The back door *was* locked. We both tried it, just to make sure.

As we headed for the fire escape, Jesse started muttering about how he must be out of his mind and he didn't know why he let me talk him into these things and was I trying to get us both killed. But he followed me up the first flight of stairs.

I have to admit — they *were* a bit rickety. It helped to hold on to the metal rails, but the steps were a lot wobblier than steps are supposed to be. Steep, too. Way steeper than normal stairs. The sky was clear, with a half-moon that gave just enough light to see a few steps ahead as we climbed.

"Don't bounce," I told Jesse, halfway up the first flight.

"Bounce? Are you nuts? You think I'd bounce?"

"Well, somebody's bouncing."

"Not me. I'm hardly moving. *You're* the one who's bouncing."

"Let's both stop bouncing," I said. I stopped talking, too. This was a ridiculous conversation.

We reached the second-floor landing. It was a platform made of metal grating, wide enough to walk on, with a metal railing to hang on to. I moved carefully along the little platform to a row of windows. Tried one, then another, then a third. A couple had metal handles on the bottom of the frame. But they were *all* locked. I tried the door, too. Locked.

"Check that side," I told Jesse, pointing to a door and window on the other side of the stairway.

He scuttled over, doing a strange crouching walk that looked familiar.

Hey! My neem walk.

"Locked," he said.

I looked up at the next flight of stairs.

"Aw, no," said Jesse. "You're not —"

I grabbed the railing.

"Aw, Stevie ..."

I tested the first couple of steps with my right foot. They seemed okay. No worse than the stairs we'd just climbed, anyway.

"Do you *know* how far up we are?" asked Jesse. His voice was shaky, but he stayed with me up the

123

second flight. I was hunched over now, one hand clinging to the railing, the other feeling its way up the stairs. The metal felt cold and gritty.

"Don't look down," I said.

"What's the difference?" Jesse squeaked back. "Can't see anything, anyway."

"You okay?"

"NO!"

At least he was answering. At least he was moving. When Jesse gets in a *real* panic, he gets paralyzed. All I needed was a paralyzed partner, two flights up, in the dark.

"Almost there," I said, doing my best to sound cheerful. The truth was, I couldn't really make out the next landing. I tried not to think about what we'd do if the doors and windows were locked there, too. Climb the skinny little ladder to the roof? Feel our way down all those stairs in the dark? My stomach did a little flip.

The third-floor platform was definitely shaky. No sense putting two bodies on it at once.

"Wait there," I told Jesse.

I edged slowly onto the landing, clinging like a bug to the brick wall. Not that clinging would have done me any good if the fire escape broke away. But it made me feel better ... sort of.

The bricks were bumpy and rough, scraping my fingers. A gust of wind ruffled my hair.

Suddenly the landing wobbled dangerously. There was a nasty creak of metal. My stomach did a somersault.

"EEEP!" bleated Jesse.

I pressed my whole body against the wall, my

fingers digging into the cracks between bricks. Don't fall, I told the fire escape. Don't! Fall!

"Steeeeee-veeeeee," moaned Jesse behind me. "Let's go dooooooown."

I edged along like those heroes you see in movies — the ones who crawl along the ledges of high-rise buildings, risking their lives. But this *was* no movie. My skin really *was* clammy. My knees really *were* shaking. I really *was* risking my life.

This was a bad idea.

Too late.

Keep moving, I told myself. No choice. Forward. Still pressed against the wall, I reached out with a shaky left hand and touched … wood. I groped up and down to see what it was.

"I'm at a window," I called.

"I don't caaaaaaaare," moaned Jesse.

I eased slowly over until I was right in front of the window. Inside, nothing but black. I glanced at the wooden frame. It had two metal handles.

Please open, I begged. I let go of the bricks and grabbed the handles. Please. Open.

I pulled.

Screeeeaawk. The window jerked up noisily, but not much. Then it stuck.

This time, I put all my strength into it. I jerked really hard, pressing my feet into the metal platform.

Mistake!

The fire escape swayed sickeningly.

I panicked. Let go of the window. Crashed to my knees. Grabbed the metal railings as the platform swung out into …

Nothing!

Jesse screamed. My stomach lurched.

What? Where? Couldn't see. In cold, empty space, we swayed.

Hang on ... hang on ... hang on.

Metal groaned and screeched.

Eyes closed, teeth gritted, fingers clenched uselessly around the railing, I waited for the drop.

CHAPTER

YOU KNOW THAT MOMENT ON A ROLLER COASTER? At the top of the hill, just before it hurtles down? There's that one endless, terrifying moment when you're stopped ... waiting ... holding your breath.

It was that moment.

It lasted forever.

Finally, the stairway swung back and, with a clang, hit the building. Bounced a little. Settled.

I gulped in air as if I was drowning.

"Jesse? You okay?"

A high-pitched "Mip!" came back. I took it as a "yes."

"Don't move," I told him.

I had another try — a *smarter* try — at the window. First I stuck one leg through the narrow opening in the window frame and braced myself. Then I gripped the bottom tightly with both hands and pulled up. The window jerked upward, a little, before grinding to a stop again.

I checked the open space. Wide enough? Barely.

Wood scraped my spine as I squeezed through. I had to turn my head sideways to fit. I wriggled, twisted. My right foot dropped onto ...

Hardwood floor.

Bliss!

"Hey, Jesse! I'm inside."

Silence. Then a couple of creaks from the fire escape. A whimper. Finally, a blue-jeaned leg poked through the window, followed by an arm. I grabbed Jesse's hand. A moment later, he was standing beside me.

"You —" he said, gasping like a fish. "Don't you ever —"

He was too upset to finish.

"Okay," I said quickly. "You were right. I was wrong. I will never, *ever* make you climb a wrecked fire escape again."

"You — I —"

"No time, Jesse. We have work to do."

"You —"

I turned in a circle, checking things out. From the moonlight coming in and the way our voices sounded, I could tell we were in a big room, probably a dormitory. Grabbing Jesse's hand, I headed to where the door should be, opposite the windows.

"What —"

I found the door and we stepped through into a hall. At least, I think it was a hall. Dark as a cave. On our last case, Jesse and I spent a lot of time in caves, so I knew *exactly* how dark that is. I groped my way along the wall.

It was slow going. I led the way, easing each foot

down carefully before I put my weight on it, especially when we reached the stairs. It was two long flights down, with landings in the middle. After our fire escape climb, though, it was nothing.

We ended up in the front entrance hall. Here at least, things were familiar.

"The basement's this way," I whispered, grabbing Jesse's hand.

"Basement?" He stopped dead. "Uh-uh. You're not getting me down there."

"But that's our plan."

"*Your* plan. I've had enough Stevie-Diamond plans for one night, thank you very much. The Jesse-Kulniki plan is to stay right here."

"But ... why?" We had already survived the Fire Escape of Death and come down two flights of stairs in the dark. What was his problem?

There was a long pause.

"Neems," mumbled Jesse.

"Pardon?"

Jesse's voice was almost too low to hear. "That's where the neems come from. The basement."

We stood quietly in the empty hallway as I thought about this.

"Jesse?"

"Yeah?"

"*I'm* a neem."

Silence.

"You're holding a neem's hand!"

He dropped it as if it was on fire. "Not anymore, I'm not."

I sighed. "Okay. You stay here and stand guard."

"Roger," said Jesse.

Hands out, feet sliding, I felt my way slowly toward the basement door. There! My left hand opened the door ... as my right hand slid over a light switch. I didn't think. I just automatically flipped it on.

Light flooded the stairs and the concrete floor below.

Oops!

"What are you *doing*?" whispered Jesse. "This is a stakeout!"

"It's okay," I said, squatting and peering around. I took a couple of steps down. "There's no one here."

My voice echoed through a long, open space, brightly lit by bare lightbulbs in the ceiling. I breathed in cool, damp, moldy basement air. The walls, like the floor, were concrete. A couple of cardboard boxes had been tossed in a corner. Other than that, the basement was empty.

Maybe the saboteur had already been here? I scampered down the rest of the stairs and did a quick check, looking for anything fishy. Loose wires. Tottery windows. I even sniffed for strange odors, like floor wax. Just in case.

Satisfied, I ran upstairs and turned out the light.

"Looks clean down there," I said.

"Good," said Jesse. "So now what?"

"We find a place to hide ... and we wait."

Finding a place wasn't hard. The little room under the stairs, where we'd hidden the day before, was just a few steps away.

As we ducked inside, Jesse grabbed my arm. "Remember what happened last time? Maybe we should make *sure* we're alone."

We separated, moving in opposite directions and feeling our way around the little room. I tried not to wonder if any second I was going to touch the clothes or hair, or — ick! — skin of a living, breathing saboteur. Jesse and I knew we were going to meet in the middle. Even so, when our hands touched, we both jumped.

"I need to sit down," said Jesse. He settled himself behind the door, which was open just a crack. I plopped down beside him. "This could take a while."

It did. That's the trouble with stakeouts. Mostly nothing happens, and all you get is a sore backside. The air was stuffy, too, and full of dust. Jesse sneezed a couple of times, which got me worried. What if he sneezed at the wrong time?

After half an hour, I started wondering what was happening in the cemetery. Did anybody notice we were gone? Did they care?

It was getting close to forty minutes when Jesse said, "Stevie?"

"Yeah?"

"I don't think this is working."

Rats! I hated to give up.

"I'm getting hungry."

I sighed. "Okay, maybe —"

"Shhhh!"

I lowered my voice to a whisper. "What?"

"Do you hear something?"

I listened. A dull thud, like a door closing. Jesse clutched my arm. I froze, muscles tense, senses alert. After a while, a soft repeating sound …

Footsteps.

I strained to hear. Getting closer?

Yes. And so was Jesse. He was edging toward me. Soon he was so close, his breath warmed my right ear.

"Stevie?"

"Shhhh!"

If it was someone from the crew, he or she wouldn't worry about making noise — or about turning the lights on.

Seconds went by. No lights.

Through the crack in the door, I spotted the thin beam of a flashlight. The footsteps were stealthy, careful.

It *had* to be the saboteur.

And any second now, he — or she — was going to walk right past the door. All we had to do was spy through the crack —

But Jesse was in the way. I tried to get around him, but I guess he didn't understand. He started pushing us both *away* from the door.

Oh, for crying out loud! I gave him a shove.

He tipped over.

Thunk!

An elbow? Hitting the floor? Could one little elbow be that loud?

I froze. My ears strained ...

A single intake of breath from Jesse.

Then suddenly — a harsh scraping noise outside — something being dragged across the hallway floor.

BANG! The door slammed shut. More scraping, then a loud *thud* as something was pushed against

132

the door. Somebody was blocking our way out.

I dived over Jesse and shoved hard against the door. It didn't budge. I threw my whole body at it, shoulder first. Nothing.

We were trapped!

"HEY!" I yelled. "LET US OUT!"

Beside me, Jesse clawed frantically at the door. He hates closed-in spaces. "HEY!" he hollered.

More footsteps outside. Quick ones this time.

"Come on!" I called. "We're just playing in here. We're kids. OPEN THE DOOR!"

Jesse clutched my arm. "What's that smell?"

I sniffed. The hairs on the back of my neck prickled.

"Stevie? Is that ... smoke?"

It was. The sickly sweet smell oozed under the door and into our nostrils.

Terror ripped through my body. I threw myself at the door again — and again.

Jesse grabbed me. "Use your feet!"

We flipped onto our backs and pushed at the door with our legs — grunting, straining, kicking. Fire! Somebody out there was setting a fire. And we were trapped in here. We'd be —

Don't think, I told myself. Just push!

"HELP!" yelled Jesse. "SOMEBODY! HELP!"

Who would hear?

Nobody.

I joined in anyway. "HELP! IN HERE! HELP!"

We were screaming so loud we didn't even hear the voice yelling back. It wasn't until we saw the light coming in around the door that we stopped.

"Stevie? Jesse? For Pete's sake, will you stop that racket?"

"Gram?" I scrambled over to the door and spoke into the crack. "Is that you?"

"Of course, it's me. How did you get in there, anyway? What's this box doing here?"

A scraping noise. A minute later, the door opened. Jesse and I shot out as if we'd been fired from a catapult.

We danced around Gram, leaping and whooping in the bright hallway. Jesse grabbed her hands and looked so happy, I thought he'd kiss her. I *did* kiss her. We both got tangled up in her cape.

"Are we ever glad to see you!" crowed Jesse.

Gram wrestled her hands back and straightened her cape. "Well, I'm glad to see you, too. But I would have been even happier to see you in the cemetery — where you belong!"

We stopped dancing.

"Sorry, Gram."

Jesse was sniffing the air. I sniffed, too. No smoke smell, or not much. No fire, either.

"*You* missed a call," said Gram, pointing at me. "What's going on, Stevie? You're not even made up, or in costume."

"We, uh ... got trapped. In there!" I pointed.

"I can *see* that. But what were you doing in there in the first place?"

"Uh ... hiding?" I said lamely.

"And seeking," added Jesse quickly. "Hide-and-seek."

Wiggling his eyebrows at me, he kicked at the metal box of equipment at our feet. I nodded. It must have been the one blocking the door.

"You're lucky it was me who found you," grumbled Gram. "If it had been Moira, you'd be in big trouble."

"Moira?"

"She's the one who noticed you were gone. One of the grips told her you came this way."

Jesse and I stared at each other. "You mean — Moira came looking for us?"

"She headed in this direction," said Gram. "I don't know how she missed all your yelling."

I bit my lip. How could I tell her that maybe Moira *hadn't* missed our yelling? That maybe she had *caused* our yelling!

"Mrs. Diamond?" said Jesse.

"Yes?"

"How did you get in here?"

She looked surprised. "Through the front door, of course."

Jesse gawked. "You mean — it was *open?*"

"They always leave it open while they're filming. They store equipment in here. The crew has to get in and out."

Jesse glared. If looks could kill, I would have needed my very own spot in that cemetery.

"Time to get moving," said Gram, giving us a little push. "You guys are *ruining* my romantic life."

Jesse didn't speak to me all the way back to the cemetery.

"How was I supposed to know the front door was open?" I whispered.

Nothing. Not even a grunt.

I don't know how Gram did it — who she bribed with fudge, or what excuses she made — but the next thing I knew, I was getting rushed through Makeup and Wardrobe. Soon I was part of a gang of night-wandering neems, lurching and wobbling through the cemetery.

You'd think it would be scary, creeping around a graveyard at night, but it wasn't. There were way too many people, for one thing. It's hard to get scared in a crowd. It's also hard to get scared when you're being blinded by huge, glaring movie lights.

What *was* scary was knowing the saboteur was somewhere in the middle of the crowd, carrying matches — and looking for more trouble.

The next time there was a break, I sidled up to Jesse. "Want to go off somewhere? Talk about the case?"

He gave me a sour look. Still mad about the fire escape, I guess. But when I started walking, he followed.

I found a quiet spot and dropped down onto the grass. Jesse settled down beside me. He was too upset, I think, to notice his surroundings, or he probably wouldn't have leaned against a tombstone that way — as if it was a lawn chair. I decided not to mention it.

I also decided to be careful how I talked to him. I'd seen him in bad moods before, but this was a stinker. Better be positive.

"I think it went pretty well tonight, don't you?"

"WHAT?"

"Well, we almost saw the saboteur."

"Yeah, sure! We almost got barbecued, too."

"Wait a second, Jesse. There was no fire."

That stopped him. "Hey! What happened to the fire?"

We thought about this for a minute.

"Do you think we imagined it?" he asked.

"Both of us? At the same time?"

Somehow, between the time we smelled smoke and the time Gram let us out of the little room, the fire had disappeared.

"The point is," I said, "we were in the right place at the right time. Our only mistake was choosing a hiding place where we could get trapped. We were so close."

"Close to getting killed!" said Jesse. "Did we *have* to be up on that fire escape, swinging around in space? No! We could have walked through the front door, like normal people — like your Gram, who isn't exactly normal, by the way. But oh no. We had to ..."

He went on like that for two or three minutes. When he was finished, I said, "Okay, I get it."

"You do?"

"We'll be much more careful next time."

"*Next* time?"

"Tomorrow night. When we do the same thing again."

He didn't say a word. Just thunked his head three times against the tombstone.

"Jesse, listen. The crew is filming in the orphanage basement tomorrow night, but the night after *that*, they're back in the cemetery. So where will the saboteur be tomorrow night? Right here in the cemetery! Making trouble. Except we'll be here first."

Jesse shook his head. "Not again."

"It'll be different. Look at these wide open spaces! We can run away if we have to. What could be safer?"

"A cemetery? Safe?"

"Sure! Look! All these tombstones to hide behind." I gave Jesse's tombstone a friendly whack. He whipped around, stared, and scrambled to his feet.

"AAAAAAA! It's a grave! I've been sitting on a grave!"

He took a lot of convincing. A lot! But in the end, he agreed to a stakeout the next night.

The neems had to do one more running-through-the-graveyard scene that evening, and then we were done. After I'd gotten myself un-neemed, Jesse and I walked together toward the parking lot.

As we passed the orphanage, I spotted something that made me stop in mid-step.

"Jesse! Look."

A small sporty car was parked in a little lane across the road. Its headlights were out, so it was just a fluke that I noticed it. Two people sat inside, heads close, talking.

As we watched, the car door opened. The inside lights flashed on.

The person in the driver's seat had short sticking-up blond hair.

Harvey Flemm!

The other one was Moira. She started to get out of the car, but Harvey reached out and grabbed her by the shoulder. The door shut, and the light went out.

A moment later, a flame flared in front of Harvey's face. There was a cigarette in his mouth, but I hardly noticed it. I was too busy staring at the thing in his hand.

A lighter!

CHAPTER

Without warning, the car roared to life. The headlights flashed on — twin spotlights with Jesse and me caught in their beam. Blinded, I covered my eyes with my hand.

Jesse yanked my arm. "Come on!"

We did the hundred-meter dash back to the car.

"Hey, you two," said Gram as we charged into the back seat, panting. "Where's the fire?"

"FIRE?" squawked Jesse.

I elbowed him.

"No fire," he said. "Who said fire? Not me. Heh, heh."

I elbowed him again.

I was hoping Gram would put on some of her loud country music so Jesse and I could talk, but no luck.

"I could really use some peace and quiet," she said, sounding a *lot* like a grumpy parent.

The ride home was quiet all right, but not exactly peaceful. At least not for me. My mind raced as I watched the whole evening passing before my eyes, just like a movie — starring Harvey and Moira as the villains. There we were, me and Jesse, hiding in the little room. And there's Harvey, in his car, pulling up outside. Headlights out, he parks in the dark driveway. He creeps toward the building. He knows the door is open. He knows everything, because Moira tells him. Meanwhile, over in the cemetery, Moira finds out Jesse and I are missing. She knows Harvey is sabotaging the building. Jesse and I could catch him in the act! We could wreck their plans. Moira races over to stop us.

Yes, I could see it all — except for one thing. Who trapped us in the little room? Was it Harvey? Moira? Both of them? I concentrated, trying to remember the footsteps. Was that *two* sets of feet?

Harvey had the lighter. I pictured him trying to light a fire outside the little room. But then Jesse and I started yelling — and Gram came along. Harvey must have panicked. He must have run away. Was Moira with him?

With or without Moira, it all made sense. I gave Jesse's arm a squeeze. He double-squeezed back. Was he watching the same movie in *his* head?

"Moira and Harvey, together," he said under his breath. "Right, Stevie?"

"Looks that way," I whispered back.

"So you can cross Selina's name off the suspect list, right?"

Gram's head swivelled a few degrees, enough maybe to pick up our conversation.

"Right? Right?"

"Shhhh!"

When we got home, I went straight to my room and fished the suspect list out of the tin box. When I finished, it looked like this:

LIST OF SUSPECTS

1. HARVEY FLEMM
   - NEEDS MONEY AND JOB
   - MADE THREAT WHEN HE LEFT
   - LURKING AROUND MOVIE SET AT NIGHT
   - CARRYING LIGHTER
2. MOIRA
   - IN LOVE WITH HARVEY
   - HARVEY'S PARTNER IN CRIME?
   - FOLLOWED US TO STAKEOUT
3. SELINA
   - WANTS TO BE IN *CARRIE POPPER*
   - HAD A CHANCE TO MESS WITH MIRROR
4. QUIN
   - WANTS TO GET OUT OF ACTING
5. SIR JAMES
   - WEIRD
6. QUIN'S FATHER
   - WEIRD

I read it over a couple of times. The clues were stacking up fast, and most of them pointed straight at Moira and Harvey. I tried not to get too excited. We could be wrong. But Harvey had no business hanging around the set. And it was too much of a coincidence to smell smoke and then see Harvey flicking his lighter, so soon afterward — and so close to the orphanage.

Spotting some faded pajamas on the floor — dry, not too dirty — I hauled them on. Radical rubbed against my ankle, making where-have-you-been cat noises. I scooped him up and climbed into the top bunk. For a long time, I lay flat on my back listening to the soft purring beside my elbow. I rolled onto my left side and closed my eyes. Then I rolled to the right. I sat up and pounded my pillow a few times. Radical jumped down to the floor. No use. I was way too excited to sleep. I tried reading one of the books Gram brought, *Terror at Cliff's End*. But I guess I'd had enough terror for one night — I couldn't get past the second page. So I just lay there listening to my heart thump, feeling more and more achy behind my eyes.

Around dawn, I finally drifted off. Someone knocked on my door a couple of times — Gram probably. "Go 'way," I mumbled, and "Lee me 'lone," until the knocking stopped.

The sun was high when I finally groped my way downstairs.

"Lookee who's here!" said Gram. "Stevie the Bear, fresh from hibernation."

"G'morning, Gram."

"Morning? It's after one. Jesse's been here twice, looking for you. We're leaving for the set in an hour."

I groaned and headed for the shower. As the hot water poured down my body, I tried to get my brain working. Through a fog, I remembered — we had another stakeout coming up.

I was still groggy as we drove to the set — even fell asleep a couple of times. When we arrived, I was sent straight to Makeup. I had to walk right past Moira, who was standing around with some baseball-cap guys. One look at her, and I was instantly awake. The stare she gave me could have burned through steel.

I took it as a warning — time was running out. Moira had hired me for this movie. She could kick me out just as easily. Jesse and I might have only days — even hours — to find the proof we needed.

But we were so close! All we had to do was catch Moira and Harvey in the act.

The next couple of hours were filled with makeup, costumes and movie work. When we stopped for dinner, Jesse did a lot of moony staring at Selina's table, but she didn't even glance our way. It was as if we were invisible.

As it got dark, the crew started setting up equipment in the orphanage yard. In the next scene, the neems were going to creep outside through the basement door. I asked Chuck how long it would take to set up. He said maybe an hour.

Long enough for our stakeout?

Had to be.

I caught Jesse's eye, and we edged slowly toward a clump of trees. As soon as we were out of sight, we took off for the cemetery. A damp wind blew into my face, ruffling my hair and the feathers on my cheeks. Leaves shivered on the poplar trees. A streetlight flickered, making a strange humming sound.

We stopped at the cemetery gate.

"Dark," whispered Jesse.

It was still twilight, but a gloom filled the graveyard, so thick you could almost touch it. Without all the people and lights, the cemetery was a whole different place. Tombstones rose in shadowy humps. Tall trees stood stiffly among the graves like sentry guards.

"Dead quiet," I said.

"What's that? A joke?" Jesse's voice was a little squeaky. "Are you making *jokes* about graveyards?"

"No," I said quickly. "No joke."

I led the way to a large tomb on a small hill at the end of the cemetery. We'd get a good view from there, I figured, and the tombstone was big enough to hide us. Actually, it was more like a little house than a stone. A little dead-person's house.

Ick!

I dropped down behind it and patted the grass. "Sit down."

"I don't think so." Jesse crossed his arms in front of his chest. "I am not sitting on any — more — graves!"

"Suit yourself. But can you at least crouch down? We're supposed to be hiding."

"Oh," he said. "Yeah. Right."

He squatted, balancing on the balls of his feet, being very careful not to touch anything, especially the little house.

We could have had a conversation, but I guess we were both a little creeped out. Mostly what we did was listen. At first, the cemetery was silent, except for some insect sounds and a frog or two. A dog barked in the distance. After a while, the wind picked up, whistling, whining, rustling its way through the graveyard trees. It gathered up dry leaves and twigs and tossed them at the tombstones, where they made soft brushing and tapping sounds.

"I hate this." Jesse jiggled around nervously.

"Me, too."

"And I wish you didn't look like ... that."

"Like what?" I peered down at my lizard skin. I had to look past my neem nose to see it. "Oh. Right."

Jesse was in costume, too — white cotton shirt, raggedy wool jacket and baggy overalls that stopped just above his ankles. His feet were in old-fashioned black boots. Not exactly a normal outfit, but compared to me? No contest.

We did some silent waiting. After a few minutes, Jesse started flinging tiny pebbles at the dead-person's house. Ping! Ping! Ping!

"Cut that out," I told him.

We waited some more. Quiet. Cold. Stiff. I glanced at the little house. We weren't the *only* ones who were quiet, cold and stiff.

Don't think about *that*, Stevie! I gave myself a little slap on the cheek. The sound made Jesse jump.

Minutes crept by, as slow as snails.

He held out a hand. "Is that rain?"

I had already felt a few drops on my back. "Just spitting," I said. "We'll be okay."

"Hnnh!" grunted Jesse. Then, "Stevie?"

"Yeah?"

"What exactly are we going to *do* if the saboteur shows up?"

There was a pause.

"Catch him in the act, of course."

"Yeah, I know. But *then* what?"

This was actually a very good question. What would we do — alone with the saboteur, in the dark, in the cemetery? It's not like we could arrest him. Or her. Or them.

We should have thought it through, I realized. We should have planned. And now it was too late because there, on the other side of the cemetery —

"Flashlight!" hissed Jesse.

Its beam was weaving slowly among the tombstones. The body behind it was hard to make out. Just a shadow.

The light danced around, grave to grave. Then it stopped. Suddenly it hovered close to the ground. Something moved in front of it.

I squinted.

A hand. Doing something on the grass.

Sabotage!

"Let's get closer," I whispered.

"What? No!"

I got into a low crouch, my head barely higher than my knees. Then I scurried to the next tombstone. Jesse followed. Good.

I peeked around the slab. The beam was still there, the hand still busy. Another dash! I scrunched down behind another tombstone, with Jesse right behind.

I should have stopped there. Jesse knew it. He had one hand on my neem elbow. But at moments like this, I can't seem to help myself. It's like a disease! I lit out on a third run.

That's when the saboteur spotted us.

Me, actually. Spotted me!

He — or she — jerked upright. The flashlight beam hit me square in the face. I froze.

The beam went out. All I could see was spots in front of my eyes. But I could *hear* pounding feet.

"He's running away," yelled Jesse.

"After him!" I hollered.

I charged forward — and ran, shinbone-first, right into a tombstone.

"Oof! Iy-iy-iy! Owww!"

Serious pain! I toppled forward, hit a few more fleshy spots against the tombstone, did a weird half somersault, and ended up on my backside.

Jesse dragged me to my feet. "He's getting away!"

I limped the first few steps, blinking. Then my eyes cleared. The distant black figure was clambering over a stone fence at the far end of the cemetery.

"We've got him trapped," yelled Jesse. "We're between him and the movie set."

Trapped? How was he trapped? He had all outdoors to run in. All we had done was make him run *away* from the set.

But Jesse and I are fast runners. Out in the open, we had a good chance to catch up. Ignoring my throbbing shin, I broke into a six-toed sprint.

Jesse was already running. "Come on!" he yelled.

We raced across the cemetery, leaping over tombstones, scrambling around shrubs. I stumbled. Hands and knees skidded across the grass. Stupid shoes! I lurched to my feet, kept running. We were at the stone fence. Jesse bounded over ahead of me. I tried. But my leg! And the shoes! I scissors-stepped over, then took off again.

Were we gaining on him? Yes!

He was still just a dark outline, but I could make out his head. There was something on it. Something high. What the —

Don't think, Stevie. Just run. Jesse led the way, racing across a big open field, overgrown and rough. Full of dips, holes in the ground. Patches of thistles, tall weeds. Don't stop! Run!

The saboteur was within stone-throwing distance now. We almost had him. But what was this? Some kind of parking lot. The backs of low buildings. The saboteur ran straight for a glass door. In the light above it, I could see him clearly for the first time. Just from the back, but that thing on his head? Sir James's missing top hat. He was wearing a long black overcoat, too. Sir James's stolen costume!

He grabbed the door. Opened it. Ran inside. The door closed.

We speeded up. Seconds later our feet hit solid pavement. We flew across the lot. Jesse reached the door first, and we charged inside. A long corridor ending in a right turn. We couldn't see the saboteur. But we could hear pounding feet.

It was like one of those weird dreams where you're running down long hallways — and you can't get out. At the end of the corridor, we turned left into — another corridor. We ran to the end. Another turn, another corridor, and finally, a door! I jerked it open. Ran through.

There was a scream. In front of me was a little knot of people — a man, a woman, a kid in a stroller. The kid was eating an ice cream cone. It was the woman who had screamed. Her hand was out, and her finger was pointing.

Straight at me.

I glanced around. Lights. Music. Stores. Benches. Crowds of people, walking, talking, looking around.

We were in *a mall!*

CHAPTER

MALL SHOPPERS STARED, THEIR EYES AS BIG AS baseballs. Some covered their mouths with their hands. They looked terrified!

Suddenly I understood. Blue lizard scales. Feathers sticking out of cheek. Hideous faucet nose. I knew it was a good makeup job, but I never knew *how* good until that moment.

"It's okay," I said, holding up a hand.

The claws only made things worse. The kid in the stroller let out a shriek. An old guy got wobbly, and a woman in a tracksuit had to prop him up. There were gasps and squeals as more people got their first glimpse of a real live neem.

But where was the saboteur? I charged forward, and the crowd scattered like leaves before a blower. Spotting a bench, I hopped up to look around. A man at the other end scooted right onto the floor.

"That way!" I yelled to Jesse. At the far end of a corridor, I could see the tall hat bobbing above the crowd.

We took off again at a run. A few people saw us coming and leaped aside. Most got a nasty surprise. There were screams, yells. I kept hollering, "It's okay," but it didn't seem to help.

We skidded past a couple of clothing stores, veered left at a shoe store and roared into the Food Court. That's where things got *really* messy. Trays dropping, food flying. I skittered through something wet and sloppy, lost my balance — whoaaa! — got it back, and we were out the other side. The saboteur was still half a dozen stores ahead.

"There!" yelled Jesse as the black-coated figure disappeared into a Buy-Right supermarket. We shot in close behind. And stopped. He was gone. Where? Five lines of people stood frozen at the cash registers.

"Anyone see a guy in a long black coat?" asked Jesse.

A woman pointed down Aisle C. We were off! Aisle C was empty, and we raced down it, picking up speed. *Really* picking up speed. My neem shoes were slick from the Food Court. Holey-moley, I was *skiing* down Aisle C!

I grabbed at the shelves. Still sliiiiiiding. Couldn't stop! At the end of Aisle C was — yikes! — a huge display of potato chips. A pyramid of boxes. Twice as big as me!

I plowed right into it, full speed.

Did you ever wish your life had a fast-forward button? So you could zip past the bad parts? Lying there in my neem get-up, buried under a hundred boxes of potato chips, I wanted to fast-forward a whole *year!* At first I couldn't see a thing except cardboard. Then a hole opened up. Jesse, looking worried.

Standing beside him, hands on hips, was …

The manager. It said so on his badge. "Al Shabani, Store Manager." He was bald with a round nose, saggy-baggy eyes and a look like he'd just tasted something bad.

Jesse pulled me to my feet. He peeled something off my face. A potato chip. Stuck to my makeup. A bunch of the boxes had broken open. Uh-oh.

Mr. Shabani's eyes closed, then slowly opened again. Maybe he was hoping we'd be gone.

"You'd better come with me," he said.

We followed him to the little room where they take shoplifters and strawberry-nibblers and other supermarket troublemakers. Mr. Shabani sat behind a desk. Jesse and I sat in plastic chairs. There was nothing to do, really, except say "sorry" a whole bunch of times and promise to pay for the potato chips. We also tried to explain why we were dressed the way we were and why we had been racing through his store.

I don't think Mr. Shabani got it. He just said, "Kids!" a few times, running his hand over his scalp. Finally he let us go.

It was raining when we came out of the mall. No sign of a top hat and long coat, of course. Walking back across the field and the cemetery, we got soaked. Water seeped through my neem shoes.

"I can't believe it." Jesse pulled his jacket collar up. "After all that, we lost him!"

"*We're* the ones who are jinxed," I said, hunching my shoulders against the rain. The neem costume was plastered to my skin. My feet squelched as I walked. "Not the movie — you and me. Diamond & Kulniki. Jinxed!"

You know that fast-forward button I mentioned? I could have used it when we got back to the set. We'd missed another call. Gram had been hunting for us everywhere, and when she spotted us sneaking into the orphanage, she was ready to spit nails. Jesse's shirt was soaked through, and his overalls and boots were splattered with muck. His carefully combed hair hung in strings. Multiply that by ten, and you're getting close to what *I* looked like.

"Dressing room! March!" Gram's voice was quivery — the kind that tells you you're in capital-T Trouble.

We'd only marched two steps when Quin's dad grabbed each of us by an arm.

"Where's Tarquin?"

Jesse looked up at him, startled. "I don't know."

Mr. Forbes's face was as white as chalk. If his grip on my arm got any tighter, he was going to leave finger marks.

"You're lying," he said. He let go of Jesse long enough to point at one of the crew. "Paul saw you leave together. He saw you heading for the cemetery."

Everyone looked at Paul. He shrugged. "Uh, Mr. Forbes ... they didn't exactly leave together. Quin went later. *After* these kids. I just said they went in the same direction."

Jesse took a step toward Paul. "Quin went to the cemetery? Are you sure?"

Paul nodded. "Yeah."

Jesse's eyes met mine.

Quin?

"If anything has happened to that boy ..." Mr. Forbes was still clutching my arm so tight I had to stand on my toes. He didn't finish his sentence, but I could guess how it ended.

Suddenly Gram was between me and him. "Hands off!" she said, using the same voice she'd used for "March!" He dropped my arm.

"Pick on somebody your own size," Gram added, pointing a thumb at herself. Actually, she was about half Mr. Forbes's size, but we knew what she meant. "I know you're worried about your boy, but that's no reason to —"

"TARQUIN!" Mr. Forbes was staring past Gram.

Quin stood in the doorway in his orphan costume, soaked and dripping. His boots, like Jesse's, were spattered with mud. He was breathing hard, as if he'd been running.

"WHERE HAVE YOU BEEN?" boomed Mr. Forbes.

There was a huge commotion after that. Somehow Quin's dad managed to yell at Quin, argue with Gram and boss a whole bunch of people around, all at the same time. Crewmembers came running with dry towels. Gram snagged a couple for me and Jesse. The rest were wrapped around Quin, who wouldn't look at me.

I ducked in close. "Quin? Where *were* you?"

A blush rose in his face like water filling a jug. "Nowhere," he mumbled. Then his dad started yelling again. Quin turned and half ran toward his dressing room, towels flying.

"Tarquin! Wait!" Mr. Forbes hurried after him.

As soon as they were gone, Jesse and I were back to marching to our dressing room. Gram ordered us along, bawling us out.

"You kids have really done it this time. The movie people are mad. M-A-D, mad! I don't blame them, either. All that trouble last night, and now you run off again? And take Tarquin Forbes with you?"

"We didn't —" said Jesse.

"They've had it!"

"We're fired?" I asked.

"*You're* fired." She pointed at me.

"Me?" I stopped in my tracks. "Why me?"

"Keep moving," said Sargeant Gram. "They wanted to fire both of you. But Jesse's face is in a lot of important scenes, so they need him to finish up."

"So Jesse's still in the movie?"

"They figure that with you gone, Jesse will settle down."

"But that's not fair!"

"Fair, shmair," said Gram. "Keep moving."

Well, I argued, of course, but Gram said that as far as the movie people were concerned, it was all my fault. I was a Bad Influence.

"I'll talk to Jesse's mother," she said. "I'm happy to keep chaperoning Jesse, if she wants. She'll be working all day, and you'll be in school."

"SCHOOL?"

"There's nothing wrong with my hearing, Stevie."

"I don't belieeeeeeve this," I said, waving my arms around. "They're firing me? And they're letting *you* stay?"

"Me? What are you talking about? *I'm* not the one who's making trouble."

Oh, what was the point? Sure, I deserved to be fired. The rotten part was getting all the blame — especially after my hard work babysitting Gram. They should be *thanking* me for keeping her away from Sir James.

Sometimes life is just plain cruel.

Jesse spent less than ten minutes in our dressing room, showering and drying off. As he left for Wardrobe and Makeup, he whispered, "Was that *Quin* in the cemetery?"

I shrugged, trying hard not to care. I wasn't going to be around long enough to solve the case, anyway.

But it wasn't that easy to walk away. A mystery — when you're in the middle of it — is like an annoying bug, buzzing around your head, darting at your eyes and nose. You may want it to leave you alone. You can pretend it's not bothering you. But it hovers there, just out of reach. Bugging you!

As I stepped into the shower, questions darted around in my brain like gnats. Could it really be Quin sabotaging *Night of the Neems*? Was that why he'd been acting so sulky and strange? Was he angry at Jesse and me for investigating?

Suddenly a whole new movie started playing in my head — starring *Quin* as saboteur. Yes! I could picture him sneaking around the graveyard, setting up some brand new accident, using the stolen costume as a disguise. But Jesse and I had surprised him. We had chased him into the mall. Sure! He had to be the one. Why else would he have ended up soaked and filthy from the rain and mud?

But wait a minute. Quin came back to the set wearing his orphan costume. What happened to the stolen hat and coat?

I poured shampoo on my hair — an extra-large blob, to deal with the blue goop — and thought some more. Quin must have *dumped* the hat and coat. If he'd come back wearing them, Jesse and I would have pounced on him like cats on a mouse. Probably that's why Quin was late — he was dumping the clothes.

I scrubbed my head hard, then rinsed. Blue gunk hit the shower floor as I let my thoughts drift ... back to Moira and Harvey. Quin looked really guilty, but I couldn't let go of those two. What if it was *Harvey* we'd been chasing through the cemetery? That would explain why Moira was so eager to fire me. Yes sir, the partners in crime were still high on the suspect list — tied now with Quin for first place.

Quin, Moira, Harvey. Quin, Moira, Harvey. Who should Diamond & Kulniki focus on?

Then I remembered. I was fired. What was the

use of straining my brain? Fired from the movie, fired from the case. No way I could investigate from a distance.

It was over.

Rats!

Gram was in a much better mood when I came out.

"That's right, you rest," she said, as I flopped down on the couch. "You've had a hard night." She was sitting at the little table, sorting through cards.

"What are you doing?" I asked. It looked like she was playing Solitaire.

"Just practicing. My Tarot."

"Tarot? You mean — fortune-telling cards?"

She nodded. "I bought them yesterday. I don't really believe in them, but Sir James does."

Out of habit, I opened my mouth to stop her from bugging Sir James. Then I remembered all over again — I was fired!

I relaxed back onto the couch.

"Good idea, Gram. You tell Sir James his fortune. And while you're at it, why don't you read him some Shakespeare? He likes Shakespeare."

Hah, I thought. Let those movie people feel the full Force of Gram — with no Stevie Diamond to protect them.

"He's got a copy of *Macbeth* in his dressing room," I added. "It soothes his nerves."

Gram stopped shuffling the cards. She laughed out loud.

"*Macbeth*? Soothing? Stevie honey, *Macbeth* is one of Shakespeare's bloodiest plays! It's about murder and treachery and backstabbing."

I shrugged. Sir James was a strange guy. Who knew what he would find soothing?

"I suppose he's feeling sad about missing his chance on Broadway," said Gram, shuffling again.

"What chance?"

"Remember that *Celebrity Spotlight* article I read to you? There's going to be a major new production of *Macbeth* in New York. Sir James was offered the lead role, but he had to turn it down. Previous commitments."

She thought for a moment. "I guess this is it! His commitment. *Night of the Neems*. Well, it's a lot of laughs — but it's not exactly *Macbeth*."

I stared at Gram. Did I hear right?

Sir James had a motive to sabotage the movie! The same one as Selina. He had been offered a better job. Man, I wished I had my suspect list. I wished I had another day — just one more eensy-weensy, itsy-bitsy day — to catch the saboteur.

But wait! I *did* still have an hour or two.

If only I could get away from Gram ...

So far, this evening had been a disaster. But sometimes even a jinxed detective gets a break. A minute later, I had a stroke of pure, unbelievable good luck.

Gram put away her cards. "I think I'll get something to eat. Want to come along?"

"Me? Um, er — no!"

"Suit yourself." She pulled out a blanket and tucked it around my legs as if I was sick. "You rest, Stevie-girl. I'll be back soon."

"See you!" I said cheerfully. "Bye!"

Thirty seconds later, I was peeking out the door.

I'd have to be *really* careful not to be seen by the wrong people. There were a lot of them.

Stealthy as a cat, I crept along the edges of the circus. Lights from the trailers glowed just beyond the steps, then eased into shadows. One of the dressing rooms was open, and Robin, the extras wrangler, was standing in the doorway, talking to someone inside. I recognized her ponytail and the walkie-talkie on her hip.

Keeping to the shadows, I scooted past, heading for the trailers at the far end. Step One in my plan was — corner Quin. It was obvious he was ready to crack. If I could get him alone, I was sure I could get information out of him. Maybe even a confession!

Spotting a baseball-cap guy, I ducked between two trailers. He didn't even glance my way.

Another scoot, and there I was — facing Quin's door. I crossed my fingers and started up the stairs. Good luck would be finding Quin alone. Terrible luck would be finding his *father* alone.

I swallowed and rapped on the door. Hard.

Nothing. Rapped again.

No answer.

Rats! Quin must be working.

Step Two in my plan was ...

I didn't really have a Step Two.

But then, looking down the row of trailers, I spotted a light coming from Sir James's dressing room. The door was partly open.

Hmmm ...

I jogged over.

"Hello? Sir James? Anybody home?"

Sir James's voice drifted out. "Entrez!"

French for "Come in." I knew that. I stepped inside.

"I'll be right with you, Tracy," called the voice. "I'm just getting out of the shower."

Sure. Fine. I could be Tracy.

"No hurry," I said, sinking onto the couch.

I glanced around. The table was littered with makeup, pens, loose change, a half-eaten sandwich, a pipe, and a cup of tea gone cold. Piles of clothes dotted the floor. It was almost as bad as my room. You'd think Tracy would do something about this place. Gram sure would, if she got the chance.

At least *my* room didn't smell. I wrinkled my nose. Something sweet and icky. I looked around. Did Gram deliver her smelly candle? Sir James wandered in, drying his hair. He was wearing his purple dressing gown. When he saw me, he stiffened.

"What are *you* doing here?"

"You invited me." I pointed at the door. "Entrez?"

He glanced around, probably checking for Tracy. "I meant — never mind. Do you want another autograph?" He reached for a pen.

I shook my head. "Just a few answers. Like, would you mind telling me your ... um, whereabouts tonight?"

I don't know where that question came from, but it wasn't half bad. Detectives on TV always ask suspects about their "whereabouts."

"My — what the devil are you talking about?"

162

The expression on Sir James's face said just one thing. Annoyed! Better talk fast.

"Just a little — uh, survey," I said. "Somebody — er, Moira — asked us — I mean, asked me — to check the movements of the — the major actors on the movie tonight."

Listening to myself, I winced. Who would ever believe *that?*

He gave me an odd look — half frowning, half interested. Probably wondering what I'd say next. I was kind of curious myself. Watching me carefully, he picked up his Sherlock Holmes pipe, pulled a match out of his pocket and lit the pipe. Smoke wafted up.

That smell again. Sweet. Sickly.

He sucked in smoke, blew it out through his nose. "I am almost one hundred per cent positive you are not supposed to be here."

"It's just —" I stopped. Stared at the pipe.

It was like getting punched in the stomach. I *knew* that smell.

The little room under the stairs. Smoke seeping in from a fire.

Except it *wasn't* a fire we smelled. It was a pipe. Sir James's pipe!

"Perhaps you'd better go," said Sir James. Blue-ish smoke hung over his head like a cloud. "To the extras' tent. Where you belong."

"No, I —" I struggled to find words. "I belong — here. In the circus."

"Circus." Sir James gave a strange little laugh. "Funny name, that. In Hollywood, they call it Base

Camp. I think I like circus better. Makes you think of wild animals, doesn't it? Lions. Tigers. Sharp teeth!" He chomped his teeth together as if he was biting something and laughed again.

Uh-oh.

Okay, Stevie, take it slow. He doesn't know you're on to him. He wants you to leave. Just stand up and walk ... very ... slowly ... toward the door.

So that's what I did. Actually, that's what I *started* to do. But I was barely off the couch when I spotted something. One of the piles of clothes on the floor was black.

A voice in my head told me to ignore it.

Why don't I ever *listen*?

I eyeballed that pile for just a second too long. Then I reached out and touched it. A soggy black coat rose in my hand. Underneath was a squashed top hat.

I gazed up into a pair of cold blue eyes.

Sir James gave me a tight smile. "It's the oddest thing. That costume was there all along, in the back of my closet. I found it just a few minutes ago."

"Oh," I dropped the coat. "That's ... good."

I glanced at the door. Sir James's eyes followed mine.

"You don't believe me, do you?" he said, slowly closing the door.

The smile was gone.

He knew.

CHAPTER

S IR JAMES BLINKED FIRST.

"Oh, dear," he said in a fake-upset voice. "I've been caught! Found out. Nabbed. Unmasked. And by a baby detective!" He let out a raspy laugh that ended in a cough.

I *hate* being called a baby. But I knew better than to argue. My eyes flickered again toward the door.

"You'd like to leave? Go tattle to Brusatti? Call the police?"

I *really* hate being called a tattletale.

He moved a step closer to the door. "Let me give you some advice, my dear. For your own good."

"Advice?" I repeated. The door was just three steps away. If I ran —

"Think about who I am. Then think about who *you* are."

Could he stop me if I made a run for it? He was pretty old.

"What do you mean?"

He snorted. "Come now. I'm Sir James Sloane,

renowned actor — winner of an Academy Award, two Tony Awards, an Olivier and a Golden Globe. I am also, in case you have forgotten, the star of this movie." He did a deep bow.

"And you are —" He flapped a hand in my direction. "Who *are* you? Oh, that's right. A neem. An extra. A nobody."

He was right. I was even less than a nobody. I was a *fired* nobody.

"So what's your point?"

"My point is — there *is* no point. There's no point to your tattling. No one will listen to you."

Right again. Score: Sir James two, Stevie zero.

He took a puff on his pipe and stared down his nose. "I could have you fired."

Too late, I wanted to say. Ha ha. Joke's on you.

Instead I nodded and tried to look scared. It wasn't hard.

"Or …" he continued, drawing the word out, "you could cooperate."

"Cooperate?"

He gave me the smile he gave the Russian spy in *Moscow Nights*.

"Keep this little business between us, and I'll get you a *real* role in this movie. With speaking lines. All I have to do is ask Frank, and it's yours."

I thought hard. "Um … do you think I could be an orphan?"

He laughed again. "If that's what you'd like. I could tell you were a bright girl."

I gave a little shrug that could have meant anything. It seemed to be enough. Sir James backed away from the door. As I scuttled past, he did a fancy bow.

"Ta-ta for now!" he said. He didn't even seem worried.

For a moment, I just stood there outside the trailer, stunned. My knees sagged with relief.

Then, right behind the relief, came a wave of frustration so strong it almost knocked me over. Here I had an actual confession *from the saboteur's own lips* — and I couldn't do a thing about it. Sir James was right. Even if I had managed to grab the evidence — the soaked costume and the pipe — who would listen to a fired neem?

As I wandered toward my dressing room, I got shakier with every step — and more and more angry. Sure, he was a famous movie star. But I was Stevie Diamond, almost-famous detective. Did he think he could brush me off like a fly?

My knees were still shaking. I had to reach down and hold them still.

"Hey, Stevie? What's the matter?"

Jesse was beside me, leaning over, curious.

Then he saw my face. "Geez! You look like you've seen a ghost."

"Close. A saboteur."

I glanced around. Robin, the extras wrangler, was still standing in the dressing room doorway, having the world's longest conversation with whoever was inside. Apart from her, we were alone. Grabbing Jesse's arm, I pulled him into the darkness between the trailers.

"Keep your eye out for Gram," I said.

It took about ten minutes to fill him in. The hardest part was keeping him quiet. Every time he said "NO!" or "WHAT?" or "YOU'RE KIDDING!", I had to shush him. But it felt sooooooo good to tell. To be believed!

"That's disgusting!" he said when I was finished. "All those people getting hurt, just so Sir James can be in *Macbeth*?"

"Sounds like he belongs in *Macbeth*," I muttered. "Gram said it's full of treachery and backstabbing. But there's no way to prove anything. Sir James is going to keep on putting people in danger till *Neems* gets shut down."

Jesse didn't answer. He was standing statue-still, squinting into the distance. Still watching for Gram, I guessed.

"Stevie?"

"Yeah?"

His voice was low, but almost choking with excitement. "Do you think you could get Sir James to confess again?"

"What do you mean?"

"Just what I said. Could you go back to his trailer and get him to repeat what he said?"

I stared. "Well, I guess ... I mean, I *could* talk to him some more." My stomach gurgled at the thought. "But what good would that do?"

In that same strange, choked-off voice, he said, "Robin."

I glanced over to where she was standing, still glued to the doorway of the dressing room.

"She won't believe me."

"NO! Look at her belt!"

"Her belt? I —"

I looked. Even when I noticed, it took me a

168

minute to figure it out. I hissed, "YES!" Jesse grabbed me into a hug.

I hugged back. Just for a second. Jesse and I aren't huggers. At least, not of each other.

Anyhow, it was too soon to hug. We hadn't done anything yet.

"Okay," I said, "so how do we get the walkie-talkie?"

"Ask her?" suggested Jesse. "Explain?"

I shook my head. "Not a chance. We have to steal it."

"STEAL IT?"

"Shhhh!" I hissed. "It's the only way. Besides, this was your idea. Your *brilliant* idea."

"Not the stealing part."

"It's not really stealing. It's ... borrowing. We'll give it back, right?"

"Well, of course we'll give it back, but —"

"Here's what we do! We sneak up behind Robin together. I grab the walkie-talkie, she turns around — and then you run away."

"Wait a minute. *I* run away?"

"Yeah. I'll hide the walkie-talkie behind my back and point at you. She'll think *you* took it!"

"This plan gets worse by the second," said Jesse. "What if she comes after me?"

"She's *supposed* to come after you. Then I can go back to Sir James's trailer — with her walkie-talkie."

Jesse glanced in Robin's direction and made an "ouch" sort of face. Then he took a deep breath. "I can't believe I'm saying this. But okay."

I couldn't believe it either. "Okay?"

He nodded. "Let's do it."

That must have been some conversation Robin was having. Two kids sneaking up behind her, and she didn't even glance around. Not until we were on the trailer stairs behind her.

"Hey!" she yelled, whipping around in exactly the second that I snatched the walkie-talkie — and a second before I could hide it.

I froze.

And Jesse? Well, he must have panicked. That's the only explanation.

"Me! I've got it. I stole it. Me!" he yelled, jumping up and down, even though it was obvious to anyone with eyes that *I* was holding the walkie-talkie.

A second later, I *wasn't* holding it. Because Jesse grabbed it — and ran!

That's when I noticed this huge muscle-bound guy in the trailer doorway. One of the lighting guys, named Herman. He looked at Robin, she looked at him, and the two of them took off after Jesse. As I stood there, my mouth hanging open, all three disappeared around the last trailer at the end of the circus. I gazed down at my empty hands.

Was there one single thing in this whole case that we could get right?

I sank down onto the trailer steps. I was still there a couple of minutes later when I heard a "Pssssst!"

Jesse was hiding in the shadows between the trailers. He was bent at the waist and panting.

"How do I ... get into ... these messes? Oh, wait ... starts with an S."

He handed me the walkie-talkie.

"That was, uh, great, Jesse."

"Yeah, fantastic. You'd better go ... before Herman the Hulk gets back."

I nodded, stashing the walkie-talkie in the back of my waist. "Do you think you should check out some other walkie-talkies? To make sure they're on and people are listening and —"

"Stevie? GO!"

I gave him a thumbs-up and took off, keeping low and staying in the shadows. One last sneak through the circus ...

When I reached Sir James's trailer, I stopped. Time to rehearse my line. It was from an old detective show on TV. The detective's name is Columbo, and he has this trick. After he interviews the bad guy, he gives up and leaves. The bad guy thinks he's safe. But then, a few minutes later, Columbo comes back. He sticks his head in the door and says, "Just one more thing."

I love it! That "one more thing" always catches the crook.

So that was my line. But the tricky part was the walkie-talkie. How was I going to keep it out of sight while keeping my finger on the "talk" button?

I tried jamming it in my front pocket. Too bulky. I tried stuffing it under my arm. Too uncomfortable. In the end, I returned it to the back waistband of my jeans. I'd just have to keep my right hand behind me and hope Sir James didn't notice. He already thought I was weird. One more thing shouldn't matter.

Finger on the "talk" button of the walkie-talkie, I

knocked on the door. When Sir James opened it, I took a big step inside.

"Just one more thing."

He gave me a suspicious look. Uh-oh. Did he watch Columbo, too?

"It's been driving me nuts," I said with my best curious smile. "I don't understand *why*."

"Why what?" Sir James stepped past me, glanced around, then shut the door.

"Why would you mess up your own movie? You're the star." Trying to stay relaxed, I gave him a friendly-but-confused-fan look.

"Oh, please." Sir James gave a snort of disgust. Lifting some magazines from a chair, he sat down. "*Night of the Neems? My* movie? If I hadn't needed to pay my taxes, I would never have considered this dreadful piece of tripe. I'm a Shakespearian actor!"

I laughed, just to be agreeable. It sounded a little fake, even to me, so I got serious again. "You're right. This movie isn't good enough for you. So why don't you just quit? Go do the kind of work you … you deserve."

He puffed up a little at that. "That's exactly what I plan to do. A good friend is about to direct The Scottish Play on Broadway, and she wants me to star." Gazing at the ceiling, he smiled. "It couldn't be more perfect! My career has been … well, slow in recent years. This is just what it needs. As soon as I get myself out of this *Neems* nonsense, I'll be off to New York."

"I still don't understand," I said, rolling my right

shoulder a little. My walkie-talkie arm was getting stiff. "Why not just quit?"

"I have a contract, my dear. Also, it's bad for one's reputation, quitting in the middle of a production. Much better if it's someone else's fault. Or … bad luck."

I nodded admiringly. Finally, I was getting a chance to act. "You were pretty convincing. How did you make Levi fall down the stairs?"

"Nosy girl," said Sir James. But he didn't seem annoyed. In fact, in some strange way, he seemed to be enjoying himself. "I didn't mean for it to be Levi in particular. I quite liked Levi. I just put the wax on the stairs, hoping *someone* would fall."

"And the mirror! That was amazing! How'd you do that?"

Sir James's eyes lit up. Must have been the word amazing. "Quite simple, really. I just loosened the clasp so the mirror would fall when I touched it. The same with the bunk bed. I loosened it enough so that a strong movement would make it collapse."

"You really thought it all through." I shook my head in wonder. "How'd you get the idea to sabotage the movie?"

He smiled. Leaning toward the table, he picked a chocolate out of the box and popped it into his mouth. I know it sounds silly, but it really bugged me that he didn't offer *me* one.

"I'd heard about the problems on Brusatti's last movie," he said. "The local crews already believed Brusatti was jinxed. All I had to do was carry on that reputation. The whole thing's been easy really, although you and your friend gave me a scare. That *was* you, hiding under the stairs the other night, wasn't it? What the devil were you doing there?"

"Oh, you know ... we're kids. Kids get into stuff." I shrugged innocently, readjusting my thumb on the walkie-talkie button. "Did we mess up your plans that night?"

He nodded, picking through the chocolate box again. "I was going to loosen some electrical wires in the basement. Give someone a bit of a shock." I couldn't believe it — he actually smirked. Then his face changed. I guess my true feelings showed.

"I didn't mean for anyone to get hurt *badly*."

I couldn't stop myself. "Food poisoning? Waxed stairs? Collapsing steel beds? Electrical shocks? Someone might have been killed!"

Sir James made a face. "Oh, surely not."

"What about Levi?"

"Ah, yes, Levi." That chocolaty smirk again. "Well, what can I say? Children's bones mend so quickly."

Was it my imagination, or was he staring at my right arm? I moved it up and down a little as if I was scratching my back. The walkie-talkie slid up and down in my sweaty hand.

"And after all," Sir James went on, "I got hurt, too. That mirror falling on my foot — I still have a bruise."

He was *definitely* staring at my arm.

"But that's all in the past now," he cooed, his eyes as cold as a couple of glass marbles. "You and I are friends, right? We have our little understanding?"

"Er … right."

"Let's shake on it," he said, rising slowly to his feet. "Make it official."

He held out his right hand and smiled.

Unbelievable.

The saboteur had trapped me *again!*

"Gotta go," I said, skittering sideways.

Clunk! The walkie-talkie hit the floor. Loud static filled the trailer. Fuzzy voices.

I dived for it. But Sir James was faster.

"Ho, ho. What's this?" His left hand gripped the walkie-talkie. His right hand closed around my wrist.

"Tricks?" he said in a horrible rasping voice. "Is it tricks we're up to?" His grip got tighter. Yow!

"HELP!" I yelled just as Sir James hit the off button.

Tossing the walkie-talkie onto his couch, he lunged in close — and man, was he mad! In a whole lifetime of annoying people, I have *never* seen anyone that angry. His eyes were open so wide, they were mostly white, and his upper lip curled back. I could see the hair quivering in his nostrils. Ick. I could smell his breath. Not nice.

Where the heck was the crew? I'd been keeping Sir James talking forever.

My next thought made my heart sink into my shoes. What if nobody had been listening? What if they were all working and their walkie-talkies were turned off?

Maybe nobody had heard a word

Maybe I'd made a *really huge mistake.*

CHAPTER

H E WAS HOLDING BOTH MY WRISTS NOW, AND HIS grip was way stronger than you'd expect from an old guy. His white hair stuck out every which way, and his eyes looked ready to pop out of his head. We were *both* panicking. We were *both* hysterical. This couldn't be good!

We were also in a serious wrist-wrestling match. Sir James was more out of breath than me — grunting, gasping, coughing — but he was definitely winning. As I struggled to get loose, terrible pictures flashed through my brain. The bunk bed crushing Jesse's pillow. Levi crashing down the stairs. People writhing with food poisoning.

What the heck was I *doing* here — alone with this guy?

Stupid, Stevie, stupid!

If anything happened, it was my own —

CRASH! The door flew open, and Frank Brusatti fell through. He was followed by Jesse, and then

Moira, carrying a walkie-talkie. Gram and Robin and Chuck were close behind.

They all had identical expressions. Frantic!

It took a couple of seconds for everyone to figure out what was going on. Long enough for Sir James to drop my wrists and clap his hands together enthusiastically. Long enough for him to smile and make his face warm and welcoming.

"Well, well, well!" he cried in a jolly voice. "Are we having a party? Why didn't someone tell me?"

More people crowded in — Quin, Selina and four or five others. Everyone stared at Sir James. He kept beaming happily, as if it was his birthday and we'd just yelled "Surprise!" His voice was loud and blustery.

"Shall we have something to drink? I think I have ... I wasn't expecting ..."

Brusatti shook his head. "It's no good, James."

"No ... good?" Sir James's smile faded.

"We heard it all." He pointed at the walkie-talkie in Moira's hand.

There was an uncomfortable silence.

Suddenly Sir James laughed. "But *who* exactly did you hear, Frank? Was it me? Or the children? They've been imitating me, you know. Sound just like me. I suppose they've been up to some —"

Brusatti held up a hand. "James, listen."

"No, *you* listen. It's those kids, I tell you!" Sir James backed away from the group, his famous blue eyes flashing with anger.

I think everyone was in shock. I know *I* was. This guy was unbelievable. How *could* he keep lying like this? After that long, detailed confession?

I glanced around. Was it working? Could the great actor make them believe his act?

Gram was the first to answer. Her voice was low and serious.

"What a weasel."

No one argued.

Brusatti shook his head in disgust. "Give it up, James. We're not buying."

Moira's face was pale with fury. "James, you are soooo low. You're lower than ... than ..."

"A snake's belly?" said Jesse helpfully.

She nodded. "A snake's belly."

Sir James waved her away as if she was a mosquito. "Can't prove a thing," he snapped. "None of you can. I have a contract. I have a lawyer. I have ... have ... have work to do."

"Weasel," said Gram.

"Snake," said Moira.

Suddenly everyone was muttering. "Snake" and "weasel" were popular, but there were lots of other not-very-complimentary names tossed Sir James's way.

And what did he do? He stepped toward his table and started shuffling through some papers. He turned his back and pretended we weren't there.

Brusatti held up a hand. "People, could you leave this to me? James and I are going to have a serious talk." He crossed his arms, looking grim.

We headed out the door. No one said a word, except Gram, who couldn't resist one last "Weasel!"

Outside, Jesse was waiting for me with Quin and Selina. The four of us spent the next few minutes

178

apologizing and telling each other how dumb we'd been to suspect each other. At least, I think we did. We were all talking at once, so it was hard to tell. The important part was — we were on the same side again.

Once we'd gotten that settled, we moved on to Sir James.

"He was so … so childish," said Selina. "I mean, if a little kid gets caught doing something wrong, you kind of expect him to deny it. But an old guy like Sir James?"

Quin nodded. "Both hands in the cookie jar, and he's still saying, 'Who, me? Cookies?'"

"This must be a big shock to your Gram," said Jesse.

"Did I hear my name?" said Gram, popping up behind Selina.

I nodded. "We're talking about your boyfriend."

"Boyfriend!" Gram made a choking noise. "Not if he was served on toast and covered in jam. The guy's a weasel."

Hooray! Gram's silly crush was over. Still, after what she'd put me through, I couldn't help teasing her. Just a little.

"I thought you *liked* Sir James," I said. "I thought you *adored* him."

"Oh, he's cute," said Gram with a shrug. "No question about that. But cute's not everything. He's got no conscience. I like a man with integrity. Frank Brusatti, for instance."

My mouth dropped open. "Frank Brusatti?"

Gram wiggled her nose. "He's cute, too."

"Gram! Frank Brusatti's too young for you."

"Nonsense. I like younger men. Young, and with integrity." She gave me a searching look. "Hey, Stevie-girl, you saved the day, didn't you? I'm going to see what I can do about getting you un-fired."

My mouth did a couple of those fish moves, opening and closing.

"I'll have a chat with Frank," Gram went on. "About your career. We'll drink some tea, we'll eat some fudge ..."

"Gram! No!"

Too late. She was gone.

Jesse laughed. "Don't worry, Stevie. Frank Brusatti can handle your Gram."

I shook my head. Hadn't he been paying attention? The head of the United Nations couldn't handle my Gram!

Selina shivered with cold. She invited Jesse, Quin and me back to her dressing room for cookies and hot chocolate. It was a nice trailer — nicer than ours, and nicer than Sir James's, too, because it was tidy and had watercolor paintings on the walls. Selina had done them herself.

In hardly any time at all, she made four hot chocolates, dropped fluffy marshmallows into them, and set out cookies filled with cinnamon, white chocolate and dried cranberries. Munching and sipping, we filled each other in on the details we'd missed.

Like where Quin had been earlier that evening.

"I followed you guys," he said. "To the cemetery."

"You did?" said Jesse. "Why?"

Quin squirmed. "You'll think it's dumb."

"No, we won't," said Jesse. "Really."

Quin paused for a moment, staring at the floor. Then he said, "Well, you know that time when I ... uh, overheard you in the little room under the stairs."

"In the dark," said Jesse. Now it was his turn to squirm. "That was really embarrassing."

"I guess," said Quin. "But the thing is — I found out you two were detectives. The real thing, figuring out the jinx on this movie. You knew how to do it. And I was so jealous!"

"Jealous?" I said. "Of us?"

"Yeah. I felt crummy, of course, that you suspected me. But what *really* hurt was that I knew you wouldn't let me join you. And I wanted to, so badly. I wanted to work on the case."

"Why didn't you just ask?" said Jesse.

There was a silence as we all realized why that wouldn't have worked. Quin had been a serious suspect.

"I did the only thing I could," said Quin. "Followed you — to see what you were doing. Try to help."

"So you *were* there in the cemetery," said Jesse. "Did you see Sir James?"

Quin nodded. "Not as close as you guys, though. I followed you to the mall, too. Man, you should have *seen* yourself, Stevie. Crashing into Potato Chip Mountain. Whoo-eeee! That was —"

"Yeah, yeah," I said quickly. "Where'd you go after that?"

"Nowhere. I waited around in the supermarket for you to come out of the manager's office.

But people were starting to recognize me, so I hid in the parking lot. I guess I missed you. Finally, I came back. Big trouble with my Dad."

We all squirmed at that.

"I've made a decision," said Quin, after a moment. "This is my last movie."

There was a long silence.

Quin stared at the floor. "I've been talking to my mom on the phone, and she understands, and ... well, I'm retiring."

"When my grandpa retired," said Jesse, "he played golf."

Quin smiled. "No golf. But I *will* start working on my new career."

"And that is —?" said Selina.

"Detecting, of course. Watching Stevie and Jesse made me realize that that's what I want to do. You guys — wow! — you have a great time, right? One exciting adventure after another."

Jesse and I exchanged glances. I knew we were remembering the same things. Swinging on the broken fire escape. Getting trapped in the smoky little room. Being chewed out by the store manager.

"It's ... um, not always fun," I said.

But Quin wasn't listening. He was rattling off the names of famous detectives — Sherlock Holmes, the Hardy Boys, Hercule Poirot, even Columbo — and babbling about "fun" and "adventure." He didn't have a *clue* about detecting!

Well, that was all right. I hadn't known much about acting, either. Not until I tried it.

Quin would have to find out for himself.

We'd finished the cookies, so Selina dug up a bag of potato chips, and we started in on that. There was something I wanted to ask her, too. But it was hard.

"Selina?"

"Yeah?" She was curled up on the couch. Jesse sat beside her, giving her dreamy glances.

"How come you've been getting so upset? I mean, *everybody's* been upset. But every time you heard about an accident, you practically started crying. You *did* start crying."

Selina's face flushed, and she looked as if she were going to start crying right then. She mumbled something in a tiny voice.

"What?" Jesse leaned in close, so as not to miss a word.

"I thought ... it was my fault."

"Your fault?" He blinked. "How?"

She wrapped her arms around her knees. "Everybody was talking about a jinx and bad luck, and ..."

"And?" said Jesse, leaning even closer.

"Well, I really did want to be in *Carrie Popper*. So I ... I wished for *Night of the Neems* to fall apart."

"You wished?" said Quin, frowning. "So what?"

Selina sat up straight. "You don't understand. I wished it at a wishing well. I wished it on a shooting star. I wished it every single night before I went to sleep."

"So what?" said Jesse and Quin together. But I was starting to get it.

"When the accidents started happening, I thought *I'd* caused them by wishing." Selina's hands were on her cheeks. Tears rolled down to meet them. "You don't know how *horrible* I felt. People were getting hurt. I thought it was my fault."

"Really? You really believed that?" Seeing her tears, Jesse grabbed at a box of tissues, knocking them to the floor and almost falling off the couch himself.

I picked up the box and handed a tissue to Selina. She wiped her face.

"Poor Selina," said Jesse, sounding close to tears himself.

She took a deep breath. "But it *wasn't* my fault! None of it. It was that weasel."

I grinned. "Snake."

"Whatever." She gave me a shaky smile.

Jesse handed her ten or twelve more tissues. "So what happens now? To the movie?"

Selina held her hands out in a shrug.

"Sir James is in a lot of shots," said Quin. "It'll be hard to replace him. I don't know what they'll do."

We found out a couple of days later, when we went back to the set. There'd been some big meetings of producers and directors, and it turned out Quin was right. It *was* too late to replace Sir James. He'd have to finish up his contract on *Night of the Neems* — the perfect punishment.

It would also be pretty awful, I figured, to have to work with people who thought you were a snake and a weasel. Everyone would be watching

Sir James. He wouldn't be able to sneeze without somebody noticing.

Word had gotten out to reporters, too. There was a big article in our local paper. It said he might be getting sued — by Levi's parents and the people who got food poisoning. All in all, it was going to feel pretty crummy to be Sir James Sloane.

Did you notice I said *we* went back to the set a couple of days later? That's right. Me, too. I got my job back.

Gram took all the credit, telling everyone her "good friend Frank" did it as a special favor to her. Personally, I thought it had something to do with the fact that — hey, I saved the movie!

Well, okay. Not just me. Jesse, too. Frank called the whole cast and crew together (except Sir James, of course) to thank us. He gave us baseball caps that had *Night of the Neems* on the front and our names on the back.

Moira thanked us, too. We found out that Harvey was her partner all right, but not her partner in crime. He was about to become her *marriage* partner. Their wedding was at the end of the month. Harvey had just gotten a new directing job, too, so maybe his money problem was solved.

We saw them again, married, six months later at the premiere of *Night of the Neems*. Jesse and Gram and I all got invited, which meant that we were in the first audience to see the movie, ever. It was spectacular! Everyone dressed fancy, even Jesse. Gram was "all dolled up," as she put it, in a red silk dress with scads of jewelry, and I was surprised to see how many people looked happy to see her.

She got tons of hugs, including one from Frank Brusatti.

The movie was really scary. They'd added creepy music and put strange bits of film together so that you got sudden shocks — the kind that make you clutch the arms of your seat. The biggest surprise was the neems. In real life, we had looked — let's face it — a little silly. But, up there on the screen, with strange lighting and eerie sound effects? We were terrifying! If I hadn't known the truth about those faucet noses and lizard scales, I would have had nightmares.

As for my own performance, well, I wish I could say I stood out as the best neem. The truth is, I kind of blended in. Every now and then, a neem head rose slightly above the crowd, and I *think* it might have been me, but who knows? Maybe it was some other neem standing on tiptoe.

On screen, Jesse looked pale and pathetic, but I guess that made sense. They wouldn't want healthy, happy-looking orphans in a horror movie, right? They'd cut out some of his lines, so he ended up not having a very big part. I would have been upset, but Jesse didn't even notice.

Selina and Quin were at the premiere too. It was the first time we'd seen them since the filming ended. Jesse got all goofy about Selina, of course. The party afterward had amazing food, and Jesse dropped a deep-fried sweet potato on her dress. She was nice about it, even though it left a greasy mark.

Quin told us that he was officially retired from acting. His dad had thrown a fit, but his mom had backed him up.

"I'm working on my new career now," he said, "as a detective. But I haven't had any cases yet. That's what I wanted to ask you guys. How do you get a case?"

Jesse and I looked at each other.

"You don't exactly *get* a case," I said.

"It's more like a case gets *you*," said Jesse.

"Huh?" said Quin.

"You kind of stumble across it," I told him. "Like ... like ... a rock in your path, sticking up where you don't see it."

"A case is like a rock?" Quin looked really confused now.

"It's hard to describe," said Jesse.

"Oh," said Quin. "Okay."

We stood there for a minute, sipping our Shirley Temples.

Then Quin said, "Have you got any advice? For a beginner?"

Jesse and I looked at each other again.

"Keep your ears open," said Jesse.

"And your mouth shut," I added.

Quin frowned. I could tell he was hoping for something more exciting. Like how to handle yourself in a high-speed car chase. "Ears, mouth. Got it ... I think. Thanks, guys."

"Don't mention it," said Jesse.

Quin wandered off to the refreshments table.

"Think he'll make it?" asked Jesse.

I shrugged. "Don't know. It's not easy."

"Definitely not easy," said Jesse. "It's tough and confusing, and sometimes you make a big fool of

187

yourself, and other times, it's really really scary, like when your partner makes you hang off a BROKEN FIRE ESCAPE WAY UP ON THE THIRD —"

"Jesse?"

"Yeah?" He was panting, and his eyes looked a little wild.

"You're yelling."

He looked around. "I am?"

I nodded. "And it's over."

He took a deep breath. "Yeah. Sure. You're right, Stevie. It's over."

Sometimes I wish I had a partner who wasn't *quite* so sensitive.

The crowd was thinning, so I wasn't surprised to see Gram heading our way. What *did* surprise me was seeing Frank Brusatti with her, his hand on her elbow.

"Hey, kids, having fun?" said Gram. "Listen, Frank and I are going dancing — with Moira and her new husband, Harvey, such a nice guy. Anyway, you and Jesse need to get home, and Frank has offered his limousine. It's waiting for you outside."

Somewhere around the word "dancing," my mouth fell open. I didn't hear much of the rest.

"Dancing?" I said.

"Sure!" said Gram. "You know. Ya-da-da, ya-da-da." She grabbed Frank's hand and did a fancy little whirl around him.

Frank stared at her the same way Jesse stared at Selina. He turned to me and smiled. "Your grandma's a pip."

I nodded blankly.

Gram gave me a quick kiss on the cheek. "Have fun, Stevie-girl," she said, and giggled. Giggled!

Frank held out his hand. "Ready, Maggie?"

Maggie?

With a cheery wave and a swish of red silk, she was gone.

Jesse and I stood there for a long time.

Finally, I said, "Jesse?"

"Yeah?"

"What's a pip?"

"I don't know," he said. "Something good."

"I don't get it," I said slowly. "I've solved six — no, seven — mysteries now, right?"

"Right," said Jesse.

"I've figured out really hard things. I've worked out puzzles that stumped whole police forces. I've untangled problems that had the whole city in a mess. Am I right?"

"Right."

"So how come I can't figure out my own grandmother?"

Jesse didn't answer for a long time. Then he said, "It's a mystery."

We headed for the limousine. Some mysteries, I figured, I was *never* going to solve.

Maggie.

Sheesh!

ABOUT THE AUTHOR

Linda Bailey was once an extra in a movie made in Vancouver. She and about 200 other people pretended to be a church congregation. Like Stevie, she was ignored by the director. She was not invited to move to Hollywood. She is still a writer and still living in Vancouver.

Other books in the Stevie Diamond Mystery series: